The sniper from Stalingrad

W. T. Wallenda

The sniper from Stalingrad

Imprint:

©2024 W. T. Wallenda

Cover design, production and publishing:
BoD – Books on Demand, Norderstedt

Cover pictures:

Stalingrad 1 © by S. & W. Wallenda
Stalingrad 2 © by S. & W. Wallenda
P.A-05 - Train ride - Eating at the sliding door
P.A-0060-Landser before combat deployment
P.A-0048-two soldiers in winter camouflage with carbine

ISBN: 978-3-7597-2058-0

1st edition 2017 "Der Scharfschütze von Stalingrad",
Wolfgang Wallenda, ISBN: 978-3-7448-9455-5

"The average German soldier in the Second World War ... did not normally fight believing in the National Socialist ideology - in fact, in In many cases, the opposite is probably closer to the truth."

Dr. van Creveld, Professor of History
at the Hebrew University in Jerusalem
in his book "Kampfkraft"

"Shocked, our people stand before the downfall of the men of Stalingrad."

Kurt Huber, (1893-1943)
German professor of musicology and psychology, folk song researcher and member of the "White Rose" resistance group
about the Battle of Stalingrad,
in the last, VI. Leaflet of the "White Rose"

Introduction

When one reads about "Stalingrad" and "snipers", one inevitably thinks of a legendary story, namely the duel between the Russian sniper Vasily Grigoryevich Saizev and the imaginary figure of the German officer Major König.

However, in this book this legend is not further questioned or presented in a new version. However, in order not to ignore "the duel", the following article provides some clarification.

Vasily Grigoryevich Saizev

Vasily Grigoryevich Saizev *(Russian Василий Григорьевич Зайцев, wiss. Transliteration Vasilij Grigor'evič Zajcev; * March 23, 1915 in Jeleninskoye, Orenburg Governorate; † December 15, 1991 in Kiev)* was a Soviet sniper during the Second World War. He particularly distinguished himself during the Battle of Stalingrad and was the subject of several books, films and computer games.

Life

Saizev grew up as the son of a shepherd in the Urals. He learned to use a rifle at an early age while hunting. After the German attack on the Soviet Union began, Saizev joined the Soviet army, where he was assigned to administration.

In the late summer of 1942, he volunteered for service at the front and was assigned to the 1047th Rifle Regiment of the 284th Rifle Division. This was part of the 62nd Army at Stalingrad. According to Soviet sources, Saizev killed a total of 225 German soldiers as a sniper during the Battle of Stalingrad between November 10 and December 17, 1942. According to Saizev's own statements, 27 more were added to this number by January 1943.

Saizev grew up as the son of a shepherd in the Urals. He learned to use a rifle at an early age while hunting. After the German attack on the Soviet Union began, Saizev joined the Soviet army, where he was assigned to administration.

In the late summer of 1942, he volunteered for service at the front and was assigned to the 1047th Rifle Regiment of the 284th Rifle Division. This was part of the 62nd Army at Stalingrad. According to Soviet sources, Saizev killed a total of 225 German soldiers as a sniper during the Battle of Stalingrad between November 10 and December 17, 1942. According to Saizev's own statements, 27 more were added to this number by January 1943.

Soviet war correspondents reported that Saizev killed 40 Germans with precision marksmanship in the first ten days after his unit landed on the west bank of the Volga,[1] and that he ran a sniper school[2] in the ruins of the "Lazur" chemical factory, where he trained 28 soldiers who in turn allegedly killed 3,000 German soldiers.

Saizev was wounded by a land mine. He was made a Hero of the Soviet Union on February 22, 1943, for his actions.

After his recovery, Saizev continued to serve at the front. He reached the rank of captain by 1945 and was also awarded the Order of Lenin, the Order of the Red Banner, the Order of Patriotic War (1st class), the Medal "For the Defense of Stalingrad" and the Medal "Victory over Germany". After the war, he managed a factory in Kiev until his death on December 15, 1991, at the age of 76.

Quote

Saizev's famous quote about the situation of the Soviet defenders in Stalingrad:

"There is no land for us beyond the Volga[4]."

Some sources erroneously attribute this quote to the commander of the 13th Guards Rifle Division, Alexander Ilyich Rodimtsev.

Reception

Saizev was already celebrated by Soviet propaganda during the war. An encounter in Stalingrad with an unknown but "very capable sniper," as Saizev noted in his biography, was glorified by Soviet propaganda of the time as a duel lasting several days.

According to this, a certain Major Koenig, head of a German sniper school in Zossen, was sent to Stalingrad by superior orders to find and liquidate Saizev. Colonel Batyuk, commander of the 284th Rifle Division, then personally ordered Saizev to study Major König's working methods, camouflage, and shooting habits in order to target him.[2] The alleged duel between Saizev and Major König was presented as a kind of personalized individual warfare in the midst of the mass battle of Stalingrad. Using binoculars and telescopes, Saizev, his observer and group sniper Nikolai Kulikov, and the agitprop political commissar Danilov spent days searching the battlefield for traces and any changes in Major Koenig's terrain.

Only when Danilov left his cover and was wounded in the shoulder by an enemy sniper did Major Koenig reveal himself. Saizev is said to have suspected König either in a dugout with taped observation slits, a piece of sheet iron, or a pile of bricks. Kulikov fired a blind shot to trick König into revealing his position. In order to deceive them, Kulikov lifted his steel helmet from the trench position and imitated a cry of pain after König's shot. Major Koenig then rose from his hiding place and was killed by Saizev with a shot to the head.

This duel was mentioned only by Soviet sources,[6] there is no mention of Major Erwin König in the records of the German Wehrmacht. In addition, the job of sniper in the German army was considered "unworthy" of an officer and was usually performed by enlisted men. Even the most successful and highly decorated snipers in the Wehrmacht, Matthäus Hetzenauer and Friedrich Pein, never rose above the rank of corporal and sergeant, respectively.

As early as 1973, the author William Craig (1929-1997) published a description of the sniper duel in the West in his book Enemy at the Gates - The Battle for Stalingrad. Saizev himself finally published his memoirs in 1981,[7] and after Saizev's story was first told in the movie Ангелы Смерти (Angel of Death),[8] the Western media began to take up the subject again. In 1998, author Antony Beevor concluded in his book Stalingrad that the story was essentially fictional, despite some real-life references,[9] but a year later the novel War of the Rats by David L. Robbins was published, in which the duel was again a central motif,[10] which in turn formed the basis for the 2001 film Duel - Enemy at the Gates by Jean-Jacques Annaud, in which Saizev's role was played by Jude Law.

In 2006, in accordance with his last wishes, Saizev's remains were reburied on Mamayev Hill next to the Stalingrad Memorial in Volgograd. His Mosin Nagant rifle, which bears a patriotic inscription, is also on display in a state museum there.

Individual references

1. Major John Plaster: The Ultimate Sniper, in www.snipersparadise.com/history/vasili.htm
2. William E. Craig: The Battle of Stalingrad, Factual Report. 8th edition. Heyne, Munich 1991 (original title: Enemy at the gates, The Battle for Stalingrad, translated by Ursula Gmelin and Heinrich Graf von Einsiedel), ISBN 3-453-00787-5, p. 114.
3. http://www.spiritus-temporis.com/vasily-grigoryevich-zaitsev/
4. Nikolai Krylov: Stalingrad. Die entscheidende Schlacht des Zweiten Weltkriegs, Paul Rugenstein Verlag, Cologne 1981, ISBN 3-7609-0624-9, p. 174.
5. William E. Craig: The Battle of Stalingrad. Factual report, 8th edition. Heyne, Munich 1991 (original title: Enemy at the gates, The Battle for Stalingrad, translated by Ursula Gmelin and Heinrich Graf von Einsiedel), ISBN 3-453-00787-5, pp. 119-122.
6. http://www.russian-mosin-nagant.com/

7. В. Г. Зайцев: За Волгой земли для нас не было - Записки снайпера, Современник, Москва 1981.
8. Ангелы Смерти, Russia/ France 1993, Director: Yuri Ozerov
9. Antony Beevor: Stalingrad, Penguin Books, London 1998. ISBN 0-14-024985-0.
10. David L. Robbins: War of the Rats, Bantam Books, 1999. ISBN 0-553-58135-X.
11. Duell - Enemy at the Gates, USA/ UK/ FRG/ Ireland/ Poland 2001, Director: Jean-Jacques Annaud.

Preface:

I have already presented the sniper system of the Wehrmacht and the Waffen-SS in my books: *"Scharfschützen der Waffen-SS an der Ostfront"* and *"Scharfschützeneinsatz in Voronezh"*.

To give readers who are not familiar with my other two books some background information on the subject, I have included some excerpts at the end of this book.

Note:

This is a fictional story embedded in traditions from various sources. Actual individual fates have been woven into this book to keep it close to reality.

The protagonist is fictional. However, his story, pieced together from many real experiences, could have happened in exactly the same way.

With the exception of historical figures, all names are fictitious. Any resemblance to real people is purely coincidental.

The sniper from Stalingrad

Black clouds of smoke hung over the city and mingled with the slowly falling darkness. An acrid stench crept through the streets. Sometimes thick and opaque, at other times thin, dark, black veils of fog. It was a mixture of gunpowder smoke and the fumes of smoldering fires. If you caught too much of it, it scratched your throat and burned your lungs.

We heard the constant rumble of artillery. Every now and then there was a rumble. When heavy shells exploded near us, some lime and dust trickled down from the cellar ceiling.

"That's the Russians."

"No, it's our own fat suitcases. I guess they'll hit over at Mamai Hill."

"Three weeks ago they said Stalingrad would fall quickly. Now the Russians are still sending division after division across the Volga. I don't like it. It seems to be a cursed nest, this Stalingrad."

I listened attentively to the conversation between Sergeant Kremer and Obergefreiter Zerberich, whom everyone called Zerbi. They spoke in muffled voices that sounded strangely rough and dry.

We could neither go forward nor retreat. We had been trapped for almost 24 hours. We took shelter in the basement of a half-destroyed house.

"Someone had been here before," we realized, as we found a working carboy lamp and a lot of garbage. Mostly empty tin cans and Oberst and Juno cigarette butts.

Our group consisted of seven people. Half an hour ago there were nine of us. In Stalingrad death comes quickly and strikes mercilessly. Our situation was fatal. Our canteens were empty. Thirst plagued us.

I wondered how we had gotten into this situation and why it had taken so long for the rest of the company to follow and for us to clear the entire road of Russians and finally push them all the way across the Volga. Thoughts raced through my mind. The order was to take the workers' settlement and push the Russians across the Volga.

Damn, it can't be that hard. We are the most powerful army in the world. Why do Russian soldiers fight so hard for every house? How did it come to this? The attack had gone well at first.

"Finally, the order was given: "Hold your position!

That's exactly what we did. Our platoon, or what was left of it, had taken the first house on the street. We were in the basement, a group somewhere upstairs. Our lieutenant was there with the rest of the platoon. There were two machine gun nests in the house next door and they controlled the street. There were also a couple of sappers squatting in one of the neighboring houses. I couldn't tell where exactly. Every now and then the shells of one of our anti-tank guns, which had also taken up position near us, would die on the Russians over there. Either the sappers or the crew of the Pak had shot down two T-34s yesterday. The wreckage of the two tanks blocked the road and made it impossible for other vehicles to move forward.

"You need heavy equipment to remove them," said Sergeant Kremer.

A stalemate had developed between the brown-uniformed Russians and us. We were squatting here, diagonally opposite the Ivan. The fatal thing about our position was that we stuck out like the tip of a lance into the territory occupied by the Russians. Only a narrow strip, visible to the enemy, connected us with the company.

The Ivan had tried to advance several times, but each attack was immediately stopped by heavy fire from our two MG 42s and a few grenades from the Pak. In addition, the engineers had laid a few booby traps during the night, which the Russians promptly walked into. There were still five or six bodies in the street and in the rubble of the ruined houses.

When I asked Meier this morning why the Russians didn't send a parliamentarian with a white flag to retrieve the fallen, he just laughed briefly and whispered to me: "There has been no mercy since the Feodosia massacres! The war on the Eastern Front has become hard and cold. We kill the Russians, the Russians take revenge and kill us. Then we take revenge again. Everything is building up. Humanity is long dead. This war is about survival. I saw things during the advance that I should never have seen."

"Like what?"

Meier had looked around carefully, none of his comrades were listening to us. He came closer and almost breathed the words into my ear.

"We are not only soldiers, we are also tools of the devil. Thousands have been executed. I saw it with my own eyes during the advance, and I don't think it was only partisans who stood in front of the barrels of our machine guns. There were women and children! Comrade, we are no longer fighting to create a just world, we are fighting to prevent the enemy from coming into the Reich and doing the same to our civilian population.

I was shocked. Meier's words were harsh. He was a reasonable and righteous man. I knew he wasn't lying, and that made me think.

Meier had volunteered when Kremer asked who would take the canteens, go to the back and get water. "With a little luck, you'll bring the food carriers or reinforcements," the team leader had said goodbye to him.

Minutes later it happened. A single shot rang out. In a battle for a city, in a war of carnage, that in itself is nothing special, and yet that shot spread more fear and terror than thousands of shots fired during the battle for that street. That one shot ended the life of Private Herbert Meier.

"Sniper," Weinberger had blurted out more than he had said.

Goose bumps covered my body. Fear and sadness settled over me like a dark shadow. I was deeply affected. With Meier, I lost not only a comrade, but for the first time in this war, a friend. I knew the picture of his wife. He showed it to me with pride in his eyes, only to immediately hold up the picture of his daughter next to it. "And when I get leave for Christmas, we'll make sure we have a son," he laughed as he showed it to me for the last time last night in the light of the carbolamp.

Now he lay among the ruins of the dying Russian city whose name would become synonymous with fear, horror, hellish agony, and death.

Stalingrad.

"It wasn't necessarily a sniper. Maybe it was just an ordinary Ivan running in front of Meier's rifle," Zerbi reassured us.

Kremer immediately spoke up. "Without water, we'll die of thirst in two days. Lieutenant Huebner has ordered one of us to fetch water, and we will do it."

Silence.

"Who wants to try now? Anyone else volunteer?"

14

"I'll go," Richard raised his hand.

I didn't know Richard Wagner very well. He was quite introverted and regularly shut himself off. Without turning around, Wagner crawled out of the basement hole, crawled a few feet behind a pile of rubble, and paused for a moment. Then he jumped up and zigzagged through the rubble. The soldier skillfully used every opportunity for cover that presented itself. Like everyone else, I watched in awe.

"He's good. He can do it," Sergeant Kremer muttered into his stubbly beard.

There must have been more hope than faith in that sentence, because as soon as the soldier said it, he turned to me, looked at me for a while, and finally shook his head.

At first I couldn't interpret the gesture, but then I knew. Kremer was waiting for his next shot.

Getting water is a suicide mission, I thought.

"He made it to Meier," Weinberger whispered.

There was no need to tell us, because except for Kremer, everyone was still watching the scene unfold before our eyes.

Kremer had rolled a cigarette. A match was lit. The tobacco began to smolder. With the first strong puff, the head hunter's face lit up orange-red.

"He'll make it," he muttered again and blew out the smoke.

In the pale light of the carbide sparkler, a small, billowing cloud of bluish mist could be seen moving slowly toward the basement window.

A ball of light whizzed upward. The artificial magnesium light flickered, illuminating the ruins of destroyed Stalingrad.

Tsaritsyn was the name of the city that stretched along the mighty Volga River for about 40 kilometers until 1925. After the Russian Civil War, it was renamed Stalingrad in honor of Joseph Stalin.

To the north were the workers' settlements, bordering the mighty industrial district with its large factories. A range of hills to the west and the Volga River to the east formed a natural boundary. Numerous Balkas, deep erosion gorges, stretched from the steppe through Stalingrad to the Volga.

Due to its location between the Don and the Volga, the city had always been an important center of trade.

Now it had grotesquely become the center of the German-Soviet war. Hitler wanted to take it by force, Stalin wanted to hold it at all costs. We were caught in the middle.

On August 23, 1942, Stalingrad experienced the heaviest air raid in the history of the Soviet Union. The sky turned almost dark as the German Luftwaffe roared overhead with its He 111 and Ju 88 bombers, accompanied by Stukas, Messerschmidt and Focke-Wulff fighters. The roar of the heavy propeller engines heralded the inferno. Tons of bombs were unloaded. One carpet of bombs followed another. The sirens of the dive bombers also caused unforgettable psychological terror among the civilian population.

Columns of smoke shot up. Factory and residential buildings collapsed. Death and destruction came to the city on the Volga. Even the hospital was hit by several bombs. Burning oil poured into the Volga. Incendiary bombs also caused a conflagration. The civilians thought they were in hell, but all this was just a bitter foretaste of the real hell. The hell of Stalingrad. An estimated 40,000 inhabitants died in the days of bombing. They were torn to pieces, crushed by rubble, burned to death or suffocated in the smoke of the fires.

At the same time, the front of the 6th Army, led by General Paulus, was rolling toward the city on the Volga. The young men smiled confidently for the cameras of their comrades or of Wehrmacht propaganda. Blond hair blew in the wind on the Don steppe. Tanks plowed through the countryside, dragging long clouds of dust in their wake. Infantrymen, seemingly in the best of moods, marched toward Stalingrad, the city that would be their cruel destiny. Hell made no exceptions. It tormented Russians and Germans, civilians and soldiers alike.

The Landser, in whom we had placed all our hopes for water, immediately threw himself to the ground.

"I saw him take all the water bottles from Meier," Weinberger said next.

"Meier was a good guy," the sergeant said. "It always gets the good guys."

"The Russian sniper must have been hiding. Otherwise he would have shot Wagner a long time ago," Hofer said.

Hofer was the youngest of us. He had joined the squad with me.

16

A machine gun rattled away. Tracer rounds showed the trajectory of the bullets. They crashed into the house where the Russian sniper was suspected.

"Looks like he pissed off more comrades."

"Weinberger, you're an asshole. He didn't upset anyone, he just shot our comrade Meier," I hissed angrily.

"Quiet!" warned our sergeant.

"If he's just teasing us, why don't you go get some water?" I added, emphasizing the "you" part. "You could have volunteered."

"What do you mean?"

"Shut up, damn it!" came the second admonition from Kremer.

Weinberger slipped away from the entrance and stood in front of me. "Tell me, you three-day soldier! What's that supposed to mean? I've been here since day one, and you? You've only been out here four or five weeks and you're already risking a fat lip!"

"Bloody hell! I told both of you to shut up!" Kremer yelled.

Weinberger took a step back. He glared at me, visibly angry. "This recruit doesn't have to talk to me like that, Robert. I don't have to take it."

I wondered if I should say something in response, but decided to remain silent.

"We're all going crazy in this cellar hole. We need water, and if our man doesn't make it back, one of you two will have to go!"

Weinberger winced. I took a deep breath and exhaled slowly. A quick look outside followed. The magnesium light of the flare was on its last legs. It would soon go out.

"Why don't we have snipers here?" I asked. "They could take out the Russian."

"See how smart he is?" Weinberger scolded.

At that moment I made a decision. I was going to take my fate into my own hands. I had always been good with a rifle. From the age of four, I spent summers with my grandfather in the foothills of the Alps. He was a hunter there and taught me how to set traps and follow tracks. Later, when I was ten, he taught me to shoot. Later, I was allowed to hunt rabbits alone with his old shotgun, or shoot deer and small game with him. I could spend hours stalking and wandering through the woods. I spent what seemed like eternities quiet as a mouse on the high stand. I felt free there.

17

My grandfather died when I was 17. After my apprenticeship as a locksmith, I volunteered for the Wehrmacht. I joined the Reich Labor Service and waited to be drafted. Finally I joined the mountain troops.

My father was a veteran of World War I and an ardent admirer of Adolf Hitler. While my mother had grave reservations, my father was proud of me. He thought I would do my part for the Fatherland and later tell of great heroic deeds. "You will begin your service as a simple hunter and soon return as a corporal or even a sergeant. I promise you that, my boy," he had said, patting me on the shoulder as I said goodbye and boarded the train at Graz Central Station.

But the real reason for my actions was much more mundane. It was love spurned. My Edeltraud had chosen another young man. I just wanted to get away from home and couldn't stand it any longer. So I became a soldier. I actually thought that as a mountain infantryman I would spend a lot of time in the countryside, but instead fate had led my division to Stalingrad.

On September 21, 1942, the staff of the 100th Infantry Division received the order to march. We were to support the German divisions fighting in the center of the city. My regiment reached the Stalingrad area on September 26. What we found no longer resembled a cityscape. We were in a huge field of rubble.

The answer to the question how this could have happened was given to us immediately. As soon as we reached our starting positions, it began. The Russian air force and artillery had been pounding us nonstop since our arrival. There was hissing, howling, and rumbling everywhere. Our losses were enormous.

I didn't want to die like that. I didn't want the building we were hiding in to collapse from a direct hit, either from the shrapnel of a shell or from the falling basement ceiling. And I certainly didn't want to fall victim to a Russian sniper.

"Robert, can I borrow your binoculars?" I asked Sergeant Kremer.

He reached over and handed them to me. I checked my Karabiner 98, a good rifle. The sights were properly adjusted and I had inserted a fresh loading strip after the last cleaning.

"What are you up to?" Kremer wanted to know.

"Act," I replied and crawled outside.

It took me only a few feet to find a suitable spot. I raised the binoculars to my eyes and looked for Wagner. The experienced Lancer was still standing where he had thrown himself when the flare had shot up.

He is very level-headed. What would Grandpa do now? The bait is out, where will the hungry boar go to eat the tasty corn?

I simply imagined that I was hunting wild boar. Wagner was the decoy, the Russian my target. I swung the binoculars around and patiently observed the house where the sniper was suspected.

Nothing! Bloody hell!

No matter how hard I tried, there was absolutely nothing to see.

"Now he's moving on," I heard from behind me.

My heart started beating faster.

"Zigzag. Now he's crouching."

It was Sergeant Kremer's voice. He knew what I was doing and told me what Wagner was doing.

In any case, he must be sitting on one of the higher floors, because he has too little visibility from below. The tracer scars from the machine guns hit the top before. Maybe he's not sitting that high up. That must be it. He has changed his position. That's why he hasn't spotted Wagner yet, or hasn't had him in his sights.

I concentrated on the middle floor. In the pale light of the waning moon, I still had a reasonably good view. There was a big hole in the wall.

Would I stand there? Good field of fire. Perfect position, I thought immediately and stayed there for a moment.

No! No hunter would lie down there, because that's where the hunter is supposed to be.

I spotted a small window.

I would lie in wait behind it!

I raised my K 98 and aimed at the small window. My aim was shallow. My thoughts went back to my grandfather. I stood on the high stand and aimed my rifle at the boar.

"Wagner runs on!"

A shot rang out. I saw a flash from the muzzle. Exhaling, holding my breath, keeping my eye on the target and pulling the trigger was a combination often practiced on the hunt. A split second after the Russian fired, I pulled the trigger. The butt hit my shoulder. With a soldier's automatism, I repeated the action and pushed the next round into the chamber.

19

"Bloody hell! He's got Wagner!"
I didn't even hear the words at first. I was in a daze.

Since I joined the troops, my life has changed almost daily. I came as a soldier who wanted to die heroically at the front out of lovesickness. My goal was to impress the love of my life one last time. Instead, I got to know something else.

Comrades who, for various reasons, decided to join the Wehrmacht or were called up involuntarily. Men who stuck together and risked their lives for each other.

Lice that spread no matter how well you cared for your personal hygiene.

I also learned obedience and frugality. People looked forward to a piece of commissary bread and a cup of hot coffee more than they did during school vacations. Everything that was taken for granted at home was something special here at the front.

I quickly learned to sleep when the opportunity arose and to stay awake when the situation demanded it.

And I got to know the war. I saw my first dead body long before I arrived at the front.

It was at a freight station, we had an hour to stop and stretch our legs. The village wasn't very big and we left the station in groups to buy something in the village. Some of my comrades wanted wine or liquor, I was looking for fruit. In the village square there was a gallows. Two men and a woman had been hanged. The unpleasantly pungent, sweet smell of rotting flesh crept into my nose. Swarms of flies had gathered near the hanged men, sat down, crawled around, and flew away. There was a sign nailed to the gallows.

"Bandits."

It was written in both German and Cyrillic letters. At least I assumed that the Cyrillic word had the same meaning.

When I saw the bodies hanging, I immediately felt sick. The bodies were bloated and had been hanging there for some time. A passing gendarme had noticed how shocked we were staring at the corpses.

"Partisans. That's what happens to everyone who opposes us," he commented, pointing slightly toward the gallows.

"Why aren't they buried?" asked Hofer.

"As a deterrent, comrade. As a deterrent. Let the Bolsheviks know what they'll get if they turn on us. Those bastards cut the throat of one of our men. Then they broke into a camp and tried to steal food. Their bad luck was that the change of guard was earlier than usual due to a change in rhythm, and they got caught."

When I noticed the grin on the chain dog's face as he spoke, I was overcome with a feeling of disgust. I turned around and went back to the car. I realized at that moment that war was not the heroic fighting and dying we were taught in school and in the Hitler Youth. War was terrible, and I was on my way to becoming a part of it. It was a road without a turning point.

Later, in Stalingrad, I got used to the sight of the dead. I saw shot soldiers, burned bodies, mutilated people. Most of them were in uniform. But I also saw dead children and women. Victims of bombs and shells, victims of ricochets and shrapnel.

You get numb faster than you think.

"Wagner was hit. That Russian sniper has struck again," Weinberger thundered.

I was in a trance as I stood up and shouldered my rifle. Then I tied the leather strap of the binoculars around my neck and dangled them in front of my chest. "I've got him for sure," I groaned subconsciously and marched off. "I'm going to get some water," I added, swaying a little. My knees were weak. Probably for the first time in my life, I had deliberately shot and wounded or killed a human being. I felt neither satisfaction nor melancholy. I was empty. My thoughts did not allow a picture to form.

"Stop!" I heard, but I didn't pay attention to the order.

When I was level with Meier, I knelt down.

Shot in the head!

I opened my blouse and tore off the bottom half of the badge. Then I got up and walked over to Wagner. Again I knelt down, noticed that my head had been hit, pulled out the dog tag on the thin chain, broke it off and put it with the other one in the breast pocket of my blouse. Then I grabbed the canteens, grabbed the leather straps and ran.

Behind me, our two machine-gun crews fired a few rounds from their weapons. They were probably trying to set up some kind of barrage to give me at least a small chance of survival.

Without realizing it, I had started a race against death. I hurried through the ruins. My knucklebow cups searched for a secure grip in the tangle of stones, wooden beams, and pieces of iron. The short bursts of gunfire died down. I scurried into the next side street, stopped, and leaned against the wall of the house. My chest rose and fell rapidly. I was fighting for oxygen. At the same time, a slight feeling of euphoria spread.

I've made it! I can get water for my comrades.

After a short break, I walked along the street. I recognized the bombed-out office building. We had passed it during our advance. Now I knew I was going in the right direction. After about ten eternal minutes, I reached the half-ruined wall that I had memorized during the advance. No one was shooting at me anymore. I felt safe. Suddenly a cry. Out of nowhere came a "Halt!

Scared to death, I stood rooted to the spot.

"Who are you, show yourself!"

The caller shouted in an Austrian dialect.

My people!

I was glad I hadn't gone over to the neighboring division.

"Don't shoot! It's me. Hunter Miller of the Kremer Group."

Murmurs. Finally one: "Come here slowly."

I took a few steps forward, trying to see where my comrade was lying, but I couldn't see anything. Then something moved. Two steel helmets rose from the rubble. The soldiers' carbines were still pointed at me. Only when they recognized me as one of their own did they lower their guns.

"You've got a lot of nerve! Running towards us in the middle of the night. What's going on?"

I explained the situation in a few sentences. While one of the two Landsers listened with interest, the other rolled a cigarette.

"Comrade, I'm not surprised that you're in this situation and nothing's moving. The Ivan has really done a number on us."

The person who had rolled the cigarette lit it and then joined the conversation. Smoke billowed from his mouth as he spoke. "But you could almost have saved yourself the trip, I have it on good authority that we'll get support tomorrow and chase the Russians across the Volga for good!"

"We'll be dying of thirst by then," I replied, pointing to the canteens.

"If nothing has changed in the last few hours, you'll find the field kitchen, the supply train and the company command post all in one place."

The other spoke up. "If I were you, I'd give the old man a brief report on the situation before you fill the canteens."

"It's the middle of the night," I replied.

The smoker nodded. "Go to the company command post anyway. There's always someone there with something to say! If you don't, you're guaranteed to get a hell of an enema from Wohlleben!"

Sergeant Major Wohlleben was our sergeant, an old warhorse and very moody. He could make your life easier or incredibly difficult.

"Can you tell me where I can find him?"

A flare whizzed up. The two helmets lowered. I took cover as well. Shots rang out. Two minutes later it was quiet again.

"Damn, Ivan, the Russian never needs to sleep!" the smoker grumbled and started to tell me the way. Then he handed me his canteen. "Drink!"

I took it greedily. I was so excited that I only now noticed how dry my throat was and how cracked my lips were. After emptying at least half of the bottle, I handed it back to him. "Thank you so much."

"That's all right," he replied, raising his hand in farewell.

Thank God it wasn't too far now, and another quarter of an hour later I reached the company's command post, which was housed in a reasonably intact building. The windows were covered with blankets. Some light shone in around the edges.

Despite the late hour, there was some activity. A few food carriers crossed my path. They were carrying full cooking utensils and commissary sandwiches. Two of them had large aluminum food containers strapped to their backs.

I must go there later, I thought.

I entered the house and immediately stepped aside. A detector ran toward me, squeezed past me, and hurried into the dark tangle of rubble. When I turned around, Sergeant Maracek was standing in front of me. He was part of the company.

"Where did you come from?" he asked me gruffly. The dark rings under his eyes spoke for themselves. Instead of his comfortable cap, he wore his steel helmet.

Again I explained our situation in a few words.

Maracek pondered. "Come with me. Before you tell everything three times, it's best to tell Captain Greiner right away.

Greiner was the company commander. We liked him because he had a fatherly manner, perhaps because he was a teacher in civilian life.

Maracek led me into a larger room. Captain Greiner was standing at a table with two other officers and a sergeant. In front of them was a large map. I recognized it as a map of the city of Stalingrad.

23

Greiner was crouched in a corner. He had a list of names in front of him and was making marks with a pencil behind various names. At second glance I noticed that in front of him were the broken pieces of identification tags. Instinctively, I reached into my field blouse, grabbed the IDs of my two comrades who had been shot, walked over to Sergeant Major Wohlleben's desk, and laid the IDs on the table in front of him.

He looked at me, then at the badges, then back at me. He narrowed his eyes. I knew that look and expected a scolding.

"Private Wagner and Private Herbert Meier from my group. Lieutenant Huebner sent me here to fetch water. Both comrades were shot by a Russian sniper. He had control of the route from our position to the rear. I shot him," I babbled confusedly, not realizing that the officers at the map table had stopped talking as well. I just kept talking, telling them what had happened and the situation we were in. Wohlleben's features relaxed a little. He took the two broken identification tags and put them with the others.

"Take it easy, boy," came the surprisingly calm reply.

"Who are you?" I heard the voice of the company commander.

I turned around. Greiner and the others looked at me. I swallowed. My Adam's apple was moving up and down. "Hunter Alfred Miller," I said, clicking my heels together like a barracks yard.

"Stand at ease and calmly tell us again what happened and what situation your platoon is in. Come over here. Show us on the map where Lieutenant Huebner is."

I took a few steps forward, looked at the map, and quickly found my way around. My finger wandered between the marked streets and finally stopped at the house where my people were in the basement. "This is where we've settled; these are the pioneers. I'm afraid I can't tell you where the Pak is. But the Russians are here, there and there," I said, pointing to the places. Then I told them about the two wrecked tanks blocking the road. At the end of my speech I had to tell them again about the Russian sniper and how I had taken him out.

Greiner, the officers, Captain Maracek and our Spitfire had been listening intently the whole time. The captain cleared his throat. "Wohlleben, do we have any more coffee?"

"Yes," replied Wohlleben, got up, went into an adjoining room and returned with a steaming cup in his hand. He handed it to me. "Drink, boy, it'll do you good!"

24

I gratefully accepted the cup and took my first sip. It actually felt good.

Greiner wrote a message on a piece of paper, folded it and handed it to me. "Give this to Lieutenant Huebner."

"Got it," I replied.

"You're going to the field kitchen now. Tell the cook to fill a large food container and give out extra cold food for your group."

The company commander now turned to Sergeant Maracek. "The medic and two men from the company will accompany this fighter."

Maracek nodded.

Then Greiner turned and bent over the map again. "Gentlemen, let's come to the end of our planning."

The kitchen bull screwed the container shut. "Ready! You can march!"

Packed with full canteens, a large food container, five sandwiches, enough cold rations rolled up in a tent, and six full cooking utensils that the kitchen bull had stashed in reserve, we marched off.

I walked ahead with the canvas tent, which I carried on my shoulder like a sack of coal. Behind me was the medic with the canteens around his neck, followed by two soldiers carrying the food container, a haversack and the cooking utensils.

Ahead of us was another world of rubble, boulders, and shell casings.

"You got us into quite a mess," grumbled the Landser, who had the large food container strapped to his back.

"Shut up, Rudi!" grumbled the man behind him.

The medic said nothing. At first I wanted to say something back, but then I decided not to respond to the comment either.

He really hit the nail on the head. Without me, he could be sleeping in his cave right now.

We reached the two Landsers who had shown me the way earlier, moved along the wall, and finally arrived without incident at the small side street where I had first rested.

"If we go around the corner here, the Russians can see us," I warned.

"Shit!" came from behind.

"Do we have to walk?"

"I don't know. Ivan's not going to lie awake all night."

25

The medic turned to his two comrades. "If we walk slowly, we'll be quieter than if we run. We should risk it."

"So Ivan can get on our backs? No! We should start running as soon as possible!"

The third man pushed his way over to me. "How far is it from here to your basement?"

I thought about it. "It's hard to say. Maybe 500 meters. But it could be 800 meters."

"That's too far to walk, boys. Packed as we are, we'll only make three to four hundred meters at the most. We'll have to feel our way slowly, sneak as best we can, and then run when it gets hot," said the Landser with the cooking utensils.

"That's what we'll do," the medic decided. He had the rank of sergeant, which was probably why the decision was accepted without objection.

"Ready?" I asked.

The sergeant tapped me on the shoulder. I scurried around the corner. Ahead of me was the usual sight. Debris, craters, and piles of rubble with pieces of iron sticking out. Crouching as low as I could, I started walking. It was quiet. Almost too quiet.

Is the Russian asleep?

Although I remembered it closer, I realized that the distance to our cellar was probably 800 meters.

The sound of the nailed buttons was clearly audible. Crunching and cracking. You couldn't really call it sneaking. A queasy feeling came over me. Fear crept from the back of my neck to the tips of my toes. The lethargy that made me walk this way earlier in the night was gone. Now my nerves were on edge. My hands began to clammy, sweat dripping from my forehead. I was sure I could see our outlines in the moonlight.

I moved as fast as I could through the tangle of stones, broken walls, and houses. I held the canvas with one hand and the carabiner with the other.

We had almost made it a third of the way to the cellar shelter when it started. A single shot opened the dance of hell. It was followed by volleys of machine-gun fire, the bullets whistling just above me, only to be lost in the rubble or become dangerous ricochets.

"Get down!" the last man yelled.

Then a flare shot up. My breath caught in my throat. We immediately took cover, leaping to the side and ducking behind a large pile of

26

rubble. I was lying on the edge of a chimney. A foul smell was rising. I was immediately reminded of the hanged marauders. A glance into the hopper confirmed my suspicions. I could see the bloated body of a decomposing fallen man. I immediately felt sick and threw up.

"Damn it, we're stuck," shouted the medical officer, pressing himself tightly against the wall of rubble.

The soldier who had been carrying the food container on his back pushed it forward. "Damn Vareckts!" he grumbled.

Pling.

A ricochet struck one of the iron bars, slicing the grumbling Landser across the cheek.

"Bloody hell!" he gasped, startled. His hand went to the wound. Blood trickled down his collar.

The medic opened his bag in an instant. "It's not that bad. Come here, I'll bandage it right away."

The Landser stood and immediately collapsed again.

"Erwiiiin, stay down!" cried the second Landser at the same time, but his warning came too late.

The round from a Russian machine gun had literally torn the German soldier's head off.

The exchange of fire intensified. A grenade exploded on the Russian side.

"Those are our boys," I blurted out almost happily. Out of the corner of my eye I saw the medic and the other soldier lying next to the fallen man, emptying their pockets and breaking off their dog tags.

When they were done, they both crawled on their stomachs across the rubble to me.

"Erwin always grumbled, but he was a good guy! We'll send this stuff to his widow."

They showed me the wallet with photos and a watch.

My stomach wanted to rebel again, but I suppressed the urge to vomit. "We...we have to move on. Our people are firing barrages!" I groaned.

"How much further?"

"Maybe 500 meters!"

"Take the canteens off me. I'll strap on the aluminum canister."

Wordlessly, I complied.

With a few deft moves, the medic had strapped the canteen to his back. "Whenever you're ready, we'll walk!"

27

I nodded in agreement and waited for the Russians to stop firing. When the hissing and buzzing of the Soviet machine guns stopped for a moment, I pushed myself up and hurried away.

The fear had now completely taken hold of me. The feeling that drove me was indescribable. It was as if an invisible hand was reaching out for me and its fingertips were about to touch the back of my neck. I ran as fast as I could. My lungs threatened to burst. I felt a stab in my side.

The two machine-gun crews fired volley after volley from their weapons. The Pak also lobbed explosive grenades in the direction of the Russians. I reached the spot where Meier had been shot. He was still lying there. My legs were getting heavy. I took cover. Shortly after, the sergeant and the lance corporal with the cooking utensils fell to the ground next to me. The sergeant was drenched in sweat. He was panting like a horse.

The fire was completely out.

When the chief hunter had recovered somewhat, he asked: "Is this one of the ones you told me about?"

"Yes," came the short answer.

"What if the Ivan has put a new sniper there?"

By now I was breathing normally again. "Then at least one of us will probably get it," I said dryly. I thought of my Edeltraud again.

It was a strange moment to think of his mistress now, I thought.

But the thought of her brought me closer to the usual lethargy of life. I guess the Ivan didn't see where we are now. We'll start running on the count of three! If there's a sniper over there, he'll only get one of us. Then he'll have to take cover, because the machine-gun crews will react and take him under fire.

"I wish I had your sense of humor," fumed the peasant with the cooking utensils.

"We can't stay here forever."

"Why don't you tell your people that we're going to start running now? Then they can fire another barrage."

"And the Russian knows that we are sitting here!"

The sergeant agreed. "He's right. If the Ivan hasn't noticed how far we've come, it will give us a time advantage. We have to risk it."

The lanser grumbled. "And what about the sniper?"

"I'll go first. If someone is crouching over there, he'll shoot me," I said, jumping up and running away.

28

I no longer understood myself. A moment ago I was trembling and fearing for my life, and now I didn't care. Not a shot was fired. Instead, our two machine guns started firing at the Soviets again. I heard rapid steps and heavy panting behind me.

They are following me!

voices were raised. My comrades in the basement were cheering us on. "Alfred! Run, boy! Great!"

I saw the entrance to the cellar and slid down more than I ran. Behind me, the Sergeant and the Landser reached their destination unmolested.

"You son of a gun made it!" cheered Sergeant Kremer.

First the canteens were distributed, then the food.

"Hofer, run to Lieutenant Huebner and tell him that Alfred is back."

"Oh yes," I added. "I have a note from the old man for Huebner. I dug out the note and handed it to Hofer.

Sergeant Kremer grinned. "And tell them to bring their cooking utensils. There's plenty of food for everyone," he added.

Lieutenant Huebner wiped his cooking utensils with the last piece of bread. "Men, that was an outstanding performance by Hunter Miller. We have been given food and drink. It shows once again that certain things can't be planned. Normally we should have pushed the Ivan across the Volga long ago, but this time he is putting up a fierce fight. But that will soon be over," he explained, packing up the cooking utensils as he spoke. Then he stood up. "Two men are always on guard. The others sleep. More troops are being transferred to our front at the moment. Tomorrow morning at eight we'll attack."

I wasn't allowed more than two hours of sleep. At 6:00 a.m. our artillery began to pound. The main focus of the shelling was on Mamai Hill, but the Russians were also well covered in our front.

Huiit - Wumm

The whistling, roaring and thundering increased.

I crawled out of my tent. Weinberger was snoring, Hofer had pulled his tarpaulin over his head, and Sergeant Kremer was lying motionless between an empty ammunition box and his rifle.

Zerberich sat by the cellar entrance, watching the Russian side of the house. His tent was neatly rolled up. The lance corporal noticed me standing up. "Now it's the turn of the big suitcases. After that, the eight-eight will croak a bit further forward, and if no Luftwafffe come today, we'll be next."

I folded my tent lengthwise and began to roll it up. "Zerbi, haven't you slept at all?" I asked in amazement.

"Someone has to be careful. You were all off to the land of dreams right after dinner," came the stoically calm reply.

I went to Zerbi and pointed outside. "I need to take a walk," I said. "Is it quiet at Ivan's?"

"You can scurry to the latrine. The Russians are as flat as we are," replied the lance corporal, slipping a small tube of pills into his field blouse.

So that's his secret, I thought, he's swallowing Pervitin.

I hated that miracle pill. It keeps you awake and awakens unimagined powers, but when the effect wears off, it pulls you into a hole from which you can't easily get out.

For some time now, it has not been so easy to get hold of these tablets, which are coveted by many countrymen. Distribution has been severely restricted for some time now.

Well, Zerbi must have his sources, I thought and went outside.

When I returned a few minutes later, everyone had risen.

"Eat and drink, men. Take care of your weapons," Kremer grumbled.

Almost without a word, the Landser complied. The fatigue was palpable. We packed up. I checked my carbine and reloaded.

Wham wham

The sound of the shells swirling above us had changed. Zerbi's suspicions seemed to come true. The whistling of the heavy explosives had stopped, but the rounds from our 88mm guns were thundering towards the enemy.

"Who has got hand grenades?"

Hofer was the only one who answered. "Two pieces."

"Give me one," Zerberich asked.

Kremer snapped the magazine into his submachine gun, then put on his steel helmet and fastened the leather strap under his chin. "We'll stay as close together as possible. When we go into the houses, watch out for booby traps!"

30

"The boss is coming," Zerberich interrupted.

No sooner had he spoken than we heard a loud call: "Out! Get ready to attack!"

My heart began to beat again. My hands became clammy and an uneasy feeling spread through my stomach. We left the basement. Kremer went straight to our platoon leader. I could only make out a few words, but it was clear that we were to storm the other side and drive the Russians out of their houses.

"Close combat," Zerberich whispered. "I hope you've got your shovels and bayonets sharpened!"

I shuddered at the thought of hand-to-hand combat. My knees trembled. Various thoughts raced through my head. I didn't know if I had killed the Russian sniper yesterday or only wounded him. I tried to put the image out of my mind and concentrate on the fight ahead.

Soldiers streamed out of the side streets. The first machine-gun rounds flare.

"The Russian got up," Zerberich muttered. The lance corporal's eyes were wide. The pupils were enormously dilated. The Pervitin was working.

I looked at my watch. Two minutes to eight!

Plopp - Wumm

Rrrrrrt rrrrrt

Grenade launchers and machine gun salvos started our attack.

"Forward!" Lieutenant Hübner's voice rang out.

We ran.

"Hurraaaaa!" came from hundreds of throats.

From almost every hole, pile of rubble, ruin, and street, Landser rose. I was amazed that so many of my comrades had marched to the HKL without me noticing.

Knobelbecher climbed on rocks. Counterfire started and was immediately countered by a massive barrage from our machine gun positions and the grenade launchers.

I believed in a small miracle as we approached the buildings to be stormed almost without casualties until there was a crash and thunder.

Boom!

Shells flew between us.

Rumble.

Screams.

Rumble

Soldiers took cover. Shrapnel swirled around.

[Rumbling]

I threw myself behind a large concrete block and pressed myself against the cold stone.

[Thud]

Something hit the rubble next to me. I recognized the remains of a hand. The four fingers were a little bloody, but intact. From the thumb down there was a single pulpy mass. I turned to the side and vomited.

"Forward!"

Zerberich had come up behind me, grabbed my shoulder and pulled me up. "Run! You'll die here," he shouted into my ear, and I followed the corporal.

Rum

Rrrrrrt rrrrt

Lightning flashed and cracked everywhere. Bullets whizzed past our heads. At one point, a piece of shrapnel grazed my steel helmet.

"Get down!"

I didn't understand what Zerbi was shouting at me, but I followed his example and threw myself to the ground. I grazed my left hand as I landed. Zerberich maneuvered the barrel of his MP 38 over the pile of rubble and pulled the trigger.

Weinberger, Kremer and Hofer came running up behind us. I pushed the carbine forward and fired as well. I didn't even know what I was shooting at, but the shooting calmed me down.

After five rounds I changed the magazine.

"Up! Run!" Kremer yelled.

Out of the corner of my eye, I saw Kremer's neighbor grab his chest and collapse. The sergeant fired from the hip as he ran. His mouth was wide open. I could tell by the movement of his lips what he was shouting, and I joined in.

"Hurraaaaaaa!"

I shouted out my fear with this call. I stormed forward. Step by step.

"Hurray!"

Calls for medics became loud. Hand grenades exploded. I saw the barrel of a rifle through a window. I recognized the muzzle flash, stopped, raised my carbine, took aim and fired. The barrel of the rifle was pulled back. I kept running.

We had finally reached our destination and were pinned to the wall of the house. There was a big hole where the front door used to be.

32

A direct hit!

There were six of us. Zerberich, Kremer, Weinberger, Hofer, the silent Zötter and me.

So the man from Salzburg got it. Friedel Fuchs.

We used to tease him that he knew everything about the FF. For a split second, images flashed through my head. Fuchs laughed a lot and loved to play cards. He had three younger brothers who were still in school. Friedel told me how proud they were of him. Now he lay in the ruins of Stalingrad. Fallen for his Führer, his people and his homeland. The letter with the black border would soon reach the family and upset their lives.

A "Now!" snapped me out of my thoughts.

Zerberich pulled the safety cord from the stick grenade and threw it into the front door.

Boom!

"Inside!"

We ran into the house. Powder smoke and dust from the detonation filled the air and scratched our throats as we broke in. The two apartment doors on the first floor were open.

"Two on the left, two on the right," Kremer pointed out.

I followed Zerbi, who moved from room to room with lightning speed. With a practiced eye, the corporal realized that the apartment was deserted. Wordlessly, he hurried back into the corridor. His eyes swept the stairwell. "Up!" he said dryly.

We stormed up the stairs. Muzzle flashes on the second floor. We were under fire.

Bang pling

The bullets drilled into the wall, a ricochet or two bounced around wildly, but no one was hurt. Kremer and Zerberich raised the barrels of their submachine guns and fired several rounds each.

A Red Army soldier was fatally shot and fell down the stairs. He remained lying in an unnatural position. Another Russian was hit twice in the stomach. He immediately dropped his weapon, clutched his bleeding wounds, and began to scream loudly from the extreme pain.

"Get up! Quickly! Go ... go ... go!" Kremer hissed hastily and charged forward.

"Hofer! Give me the hand grenade! We have to check the two apartments on this floor first!"

The young soldier reached into the paddock, pulled out the hand grenade with some difficulty, and handed it to Zerbi with slightly shaking hands.

He lunged backwards, swung out with his right leg and kicked the door of the apartment, which was on the second floor on the right, with all his might. The wood around the lock splintered. The door burst inward. At the same time, the corporal threw the hand grenade into the apartment and took cover at the side of the entrance. We also pressed against the wall.

Boom!

The explosion was still ringing in my ears when Zerbi and Ker-ner burst into the apartment.

"Two men in the other apartment, the rest upstairs, follow the others!" he called to us.

Hofer and I stayed on the second floor. We stood at the door of the apartment opposite.

Behind us we heard the rattle of machine guns. Shouts. Snippets of words in Russian. I tried to ignore the background noise and concentrate on our apartment. My heart was pounding with excitement.

I imitated Zerbi and kicked at the door. Again, the wood on the lock splintered, but the door didn't spring open. A second kick was needed. With our carbines on, ready to fire at a moment's notice, we entered the hallway. The apartment was extremely dusty and, at first glance, looked a little ramshackle and uninhabited.

"The room on the left is completely empty," Hofer whispered.

"You go straight ahead, I'll take the room on the right."

We moved slowly forward. My pulse was getting faster and faster. I was afraid. Afraid of death. The room I was looking into looked destroyed, as if a Pak grenade had exploded here. Then I saw something and stopped dead in my tracks.

Legs! Those are soldiers' boots, I thought.

They were sticking out lifelessly from behind a fallen piece of furniture.

"Rucki werch!" I shouted, startled. "Hands up!"

Nothing moved. The Red Army man didn't move an inch. He's dead, was my next thought.

I heard quick steps behind me.

34

"There's nobody over there. What's wrong with you?" panted Hofer.

I aimed for the legs. Hofer's eyes followed the barrel of my carbine.

"He's not moving. I think he's dead!"

"Then we have to check him!"

"But watch out! I've heard that if they're only wounded, they'll have pistols or hand grenades ready to take another one of us with them!"

"Do you want to look?"

"No! You found him. You look!"

There was also a brief exchange of gunfire on the floor, then nothing more was heard.

"Good," I said, first taking two steps forward, then walking around the cabinet, and when I realized that the Russian was definitely dead, I lowered the barrel of my carbine. There was blood everywhere. Smaller and larger spots or pools. It was already dried and black. The Red Army soldier had been shot in the neck. His hands were still on the wound. A glance out of the window and a second look at the fallen Russian gave me goose bumps. Next to the soldier was a Mosin Nagant with a telescopic sight. As I looked out the window, I immediately knew that this Russian had the best view of where Wagner and Meier had been shot. There was a very high probability that this dead man was the sniper I had shot.

I killed that person!

My knees went weak and my hands began to shake. I closed my eyes for a moment.

"What's going on?" asked Hofer.

I pointed to the dead Russian. "That's the sniper."

"The one you took out?"

Take him out! What a word. There's a dead man lying there, and I shot him. Shot him in the neck. I killed a human being! Am I a murderer now?

Questions raced through my mind. I had to sit down.

No! I'm not a murderer. He would have killed more of our people. I saved the lives of many of our comrades and my own.

This thought made me feel better. I recovered a little.

A crash. Someone ran into the apartment. "Where are you?"

It was Zerberich. "There were five Iwans upstairs. The house is free now!"

35

The lance corporal came into the room and immediately recognized the situation. "That's the bastard! Good shot, Alfred. Take Ivan's rifle, take all the ammunition with you and get out of here!"

"Why should I take his rifle?"

"Because you're a damn good shot, and I'll feel safer in similar situations in the future if you have a rifle with a scope. These Russian rifles aren't bad. Tough and always work. They didn't freeze up last winter!"

"But he has to give the rifle to the sergeant," said Hofer.

Zerberich knelt down beside the dead sniper and searched his pockets. Finally, he grabbed all the ammunition he found, a small bag of tools, and the rifle, and handed it to me. "We'll deal with the rifle later. For now, take it!"

Without protest, I took the rifle and hung it around my neck. I put the shells in my pocket. I put the tool bag away as well.

I'm definitely not going to be a sniper. When I see the faces of the men I'm supposed to shoot through the scope, it's too much for me.

My mind was made up, then I saw something unbelievable. We had fought our way forward two streets and were trapped. The whole company had dug in and was engaged in a constant firefight with the Russians. After one of our grenade launcher squads got into position and the enemy detonated their explosives, a front door opened and some civilians poured out. There were three or four women and about twice as many children. They carried a few belongings, waved vigorously, and ran toward the German positions. At that moment the Red Army soldiers started shooting at the civilians. One of the women ran into a machine gun. Screaming and yelling, the group ran back into the house.

"This can't be," I groaned. "They're women and children!"

"They're Russians," Weinberger replied.

"So what?"

"You can't trust them! They run up to us and set off hand grenades!"

"You are and always will be an asshole! If you were, the Iwans wouldn't have shot their own people!"

"Alfred, you can't sugarcoat anything in war! Do you know what happened this morning? In the apartment where Zerbi threw a hand grenade?"

I looked at Weinberger. "What?"

"He sent an old couple to heaven."

"What? I don't understand."

"The apartment wasn't empty. Grandma and Grandpa lived there. This is the war. Wake up!"

I looked for Zerbi, saw him and crawled over. "This is the last magazine," he said and snapped it shut.

"Zerbi, is it true what Weinberger just told you? You killed an old couple?"

The corporal looked at me. "An accident! But what you just saw over there with the Russian was no accident. They're slaughtering their own people. We have to stop that!"

Zerberich's words were cold. His eyes flickered. I was tired of home. How much was the war glorified? How were we, pimps in the Hitler Youth, told about heroic soldiers? And here at the front, reality caught up with us and overwhelmed us. War is the end of humanity. In war, man becomes a beast.

Stalingrad is a suburb of hell!

I understood that at that moment. At that moment I made a decision that would completely change the rest of my life. I wanted to be a sniper. I wanted to kill all those who sat behind their guns and killed people themselves. I imagined that I could stop the catastrophe. I wanted to jump up and run. I was torn inside, but my mind was made up.

The day was ending. Exhausted and disillusioned, we sat in one of the workers' houses and waited for food and ammunition to arrive.

Our company had been reduced to the combat strength of a reinforced platoon. Lieutenant Huebner had been put in command of the platoon. Captain Greiner had reduced the company command post to a minimum.

The heaviest fighting had taken place along the entire front. There were so many casualties that the medics were still picking up the wounded and the fallen. They were taken by the truckload to the military cemeteries outside the city to be buried later by the Hiwis.

As we anxiously waited for food, one of the medics walked through the rows treating minor injuries. My graze was treated as well.

"Let me see."

"It's not wild."

"It's an open wound and it needs at least iodine. If you get blood poisoning here, you won't be able to get medical treatment quickly. The

37

front line is constantly changing. The other day, the I-wans were only 800 meters away from the main dressing station."

"If you think so, why don't you paint something over it," I said, holding out my hand.

The medic cleaned the wound and then applied some iodine ointment to the chafed areas. "Done!"

The outcome of the fierce battle was sobering for both sides. The top of the strategically important Mamai Hill was occupied at times by Wehrmacht troops, then again by the Red Army. In the end, it was no man's land.

The Red Army had thus achieved at least a partial objective, as the German artillery could have targeted the north of the city and the important crossings on the Volga from Mamai Hill.

The losses on both sides were enormous, and the Russian commander-in-chief was informed that the German attack was so fierce that if it were repeated, the Red Army would inevitably be driven across the Volga.

Slogans of perseverance and an attack the next day north of Stalingrad were supposed to bring relief. In addition, more and more troops were ordered to Stalingrad.

From the moment it arrived at the Stalingrad front, the 100th Infantry Division was under constant fire. The losses were enormous. In addition, the house-to-house fighting and hand-to-hand combat took their toll on the soldiers' nerves.

As darkness fell, the major firefights subsided. There were only occasional clashes when Red Army soldiers who had been overrun during the attack tried to fight their way back to their own lines and encountered German reconnaissance troops digging through the ruins.

A light easterly wind drove the smoke from the smoldering fires through the ruins, creating acrid air at irregular intervals that scratched the lungs when inhaled.

I hid in a corner and worked on the Mosin Nagant 91/30. Until now, no one had noticed that I owned a sniper rifle. It was only now, as I took it apart and cleaned it, that I was confronted with the first questions.

"Where did you get the rifle?"

"Have you joined the snipers now?"

I only mumbled short answers. This grumpiness was enough to give me peace of mind. After an hour, I had cleaned everything to my satisfaction and reassembled the gun. The scope was a PU model with 3.5x magnification. I secretly became friends with the Russian sniper's weapon.

"At last! The food bearers are coming.

Sepp Schneider, a private whose entire squad had been killed in the Soviet artillery attack on our first day, jumped up. "What's wrong? I'm starving!"

"Stew with a lot of meat in it," gasped one of the porters, unbuckling the large aluminum container.

Something was stirring in every corner. Cooking utensils rattling. Murmurs. Although I hadn't eaten since breakfast, I had no appetite. Accordingly, I was slow to get out my cooking utensils. I was the last to hold them out to be filled. I figured there was hardly anything left in the container, but instead of the half portion I expected, my pot was filled to the brim.

"Lucky you, comrade. I must have skimped on the distribution at the beginning," the man handing out the food grinned.

"Thank you."

Like everyone else, I placed the utensils on my Esbit stove and heated the food. After a short time it smelled like a kitchen and my hunger returned. Now I was glad for the big porridge.

After lunch we got ammunition. Then we had to assemble 24 stick grenades and get them ready to throw. A car lamp and some Hindenburg lamps provided enough light.

The steps were simple. First you had to insert the breakaway device, then the knot of the breakaway loop had to be inserted into the wire loop of the fuse. Next, the breakaway cord with the breakaway button had to be inserted into the handle. Then the safety cap and the pot with the detonator and the detonator cap were screwed on.

We were given two boxes. Each contained 15 hand grenades. Our group was again ten men strong, so each of us got three grenades.

"Tomorrow we'll send the Ivan into the Volga," Kremer boasted. The sergeant had pulled a bottle of schnapps out of his pack and took a

39

big swig. With a loud "Ahhh!" he put it down and passed the bottle. "Let it go around. Everyone can have a sip, but please don't be too greedy. There should be enough for everyone."

"Now that's a surprise."

"Robert, you're just a great guy!"

The landsmen were delighted with the little surprise. When it was my turn, I took a quick sip and passed the bottle to the person next to me, who was eagerly awaiting it.

While my comrades sat around smoking and talking about the good food, I retreated to a corner, made myself reasonably comfortable, and curled up in the tent. It had gotten noticeably cooler. I wanted to sleep so that I could go into battle rested, but a never-ending carousel of thoughts kept me awake. First came the images of my great love. As I tried to block them out, the sight of the Russian sniper I had killed kept returning to my mind. Eventually I fell asleep.

Although the Red Army continued to attack north of Stalingrad on the Don Front, this did not relieve the pressure on the front in the city itself. Both the 60th Infantry Division and the 16th Panzer Division successfully fought a tough defensive battle against the numerically superior Soviet troops.

In Stalingrad, the 100th Infantry Division, the 389th Infantry Division and the 24th Panzer Division advanced to the "Red October" and "Barrikady" factories.

The cityscape and large factory buildings were largely destroyed. Ruins and rubble! The Soviet artillery continued to fire their shells between the lines of the advancing German infantry and tanks. The casualties were high.

To speed up the attack, the 94th Infantry Division and the 14th Armored Division, both based in the south of Stalingrad, were also ordered into the battle area.

The industrial area was defended by the 62nd Army. Due to the enormous losses, the unit was hastily reinforced by the 39th Guards Rifle Division and the 308th Rifle Division.

Fierce battles were fought for the factories and their surrounding areas. In some cases the opponents were in the same building or one floor higher or lower, separated only by a wall.

The casualties on both sides increased enormously. Within a very short time, companies were reduced to about 30 men, and after four weeks, the divisions that had been deployed had only about 25 percent of their combat strength.

The thunder of the guns and the howling, whistling, and whimpering of the shells were terrible. But even more terrifying and grueling were the dive-bomber attacks. When the Ju-87 pilots lowered the noses of their fighter-bombers, the howling of the noisemakers fitted to the older aircraft caused real psychological demoralization among the enemy.

On our right flank, assault guns rushed forward; on our left, we heard the resounding "hurrah" of our comrades as they ran across the large square in front of the factory buildings. They ran against the brick walls as if it were a medieval fortress. Some of the walls had withstood the artillery and air attacks. Windows and roofs, however, were almost non-existent.

We lay in our starting positions, sweating and panting, waiting for the signal to attack.

Boom!

Although our artillery had blown a passage into the Soviet mine belt with massive shelling, there were constant clashes. One of the assault guns had broken down with chain damage. When one of the crew members tried to get out, he collapsed immediately after being hit. A second soldier suffered the same fate. Zerbi, who was lying next to me, pointed his finger at the assault gun in question and whispered in my ear: "There's a bloody sniper crouching in the rubble, taking on the assault rifles that are lying around!"

Although I could only understand half of what he was saying over the noise of the battle, I knew what he meant. I held my Karabiner 98 in my hands and had the Russian sniper rifle strapped on. "What do you want to tell me?"

Zerbi did not react. His attention was focused on the SMG crews taking up position. In no time at all, the machine guns were placed on their mounts, the straps inserted, and the readiness to fire signaled.

The command came: "Fire!"

Rrrrrrt rrrrrrt

There was a flash of gunfire. I knew it was our barrage. The machine guns were supposed to keep the enemy in cover. It was our turn.

"Attaaaack!"

We rose from the rubble and charged forward. Just like our neighbors, we screamed our "hurrah" from the bottom of our throats. We screamed our fears.

Boom!

Grenades exploded among us.

Thud

Splinters and stones flew. Men fell to the ground. Blood spurted. The screams of the wounded mingled with the din of battle. Two of our assault guns had moved far forward and were raking the Russians. Then there was lightning and thunder. When I looked back in their direction, one of the steel hulls was ablaze.

"Hurraaaaaaaa!"

A man fell to the ground beside me. I didn't care who it was. I had only one goal in mind. A fallen pole. A steel construction with a concrete base. It had been torn out of the ground and provided good cover. I hurried across the square. There was rubble everywhere and I had to jump over it to avoid tripping. The Russian shells were like waves of steel that washed over us, claiming dozens of victims. I reached my destination panting and out of breath. Right behind me, Lieutenant Huebner ran for cover, and Zerbi and Sergeant Kremer came to rest beside me.

I pressed myself against the cold concrete. Sweat trickled down my forehead. I wiped my eyebrows. Some of the salty bodily fluid got into my left eye and burned slightly.

When a bloody hand suddenly rose from the hole where the concrete base had once been cemented into the ground and reached for me, I was almost scared to death.

Two fingers were missing, and one was still attached by a few tendons and bits of skin. "Help me," the wounded man moaned, clawing at the sleeve of my uniform.

I swallowed my disgust and risked a glance into the small pit. The soldier was a young boy about my age. His uniform was stained with blood. You couldn't tell if he had any wounds other than the badly injured hand, but you could guess.

"Saniiiiii..." I instinctively cried. "Sanitary!"

Zerbi pushed me aside. "We have to bandage him. Out with the bandages. The poor bastard will bleed to death otherwise."

All around us, grenades kept falling. Shrapnel swirled dangerously around us, digging into the bodies of the charging soldiers.

42

On the Russian side, the volleys of our artillery kept the Red Army soldiers in their cover. In addition, the barrage from the SMG crews kept the rifle fire sparse. Nevertheless, the attack faltered. The first wave was bloodily repulsed, and our men retreated or took cover wherever they could find it.

Corporal Zerberich had squeezed himself into the hole with the wounded man and began to bandage the bloody mass of the hand.

Lieutenant Huebner looked around but saw no medic. "Damn it! We have to keep going! If we don't make it to the factory building, they'll wipe us out! What's going on?"

Captain Greiner was seething with rage as he realized his company was running to its doom. The officer yelled at his radio operator: "Where's the air support? This can't be it! Contact the regiment immediately! We desperately need support from above, or the company will be gone in two hours!"

The order was immediately carried out. The intelligence officer tried again and again to contact the regimental headquarters.

Greiner became angrier and angrier. "Let them assemble and attack again immediately. This time I'll lead them myself. I can't send people out there and watch them die while we just sit around! We'll lead from the front!" he said firmly to his squad leader. "Everyone, prepare for battle! Everyone!" he added.

"By your command," replied Chief Hunter Maracek.

The Night Judge turned and turned the small screws. Again and again he whined into the microphone. The transmission impulses raced through the windings, coils and tubes. They reached the antenna and finally found their way to the receiver.

"I've got them! I'm getting a response," the man on the radio shouted, repeating twice what Captain Greiner had told him to say.

The shredded hand was not the soldier's only injury. A shrapnel had pierced his right shoulder, one was lodged in his upper arm, and one had penetrated his chest through a cigarette case.

"The case saved his life," said Zerbi, who was busy applying bandages. "I need another pack. Damn, isn't there a medic around?"

[Rumbling

Another volley of grenades exploded in the forecourt. Acrid smoke billowed from the burning assault rifle. The screams of the wounded

43

grew louder. I pressed even closer to the concrete block. Zerberich had been lying over the wounded man during the blows. When he got up, his blouse was covered in blood. He recognized my concerned look.

"The blood is not mine, son. Don't worry, it's all right."

The firepower in our rear increased. The sMGs were joined by two Paks and a grenade launcher squad. The barrage increased. Moments later, a medic plopped down on the tarmac behind us. "Damn, my knee," he cursed, rubbing it with his hand. Then he crawled over to Zerbi and the wounded man. The corporal left the hole, the medic took his place and looked at the wounds and bandages. Two porters came running up. They hurried over the rubble. Their Red Cross armbands might have protected them from merciful snipers, if there were any, and the infantrymen's rifle bullets, but the splinters and shrapnel didn't stop them either.

"Here, swallow this," he said to the wounded man, who was still bravely fighting the pain. "This will help you. You'll feel less pain in a minute."

He put a tablet in his mouth, unscrewed his canteen and gave him a drink. It took the soldier three tries to swallow the tablet.

"The bandages look good. Take him to the casualty nest and get him to the unit area as soon as possible!"

The medic grabbed hold of the wounded man and lifted him up, while one of the porters grabbed his legs. With a jerk, followed by a scream of pain, they lifted him out of the hole and placed him on the stretcher. The porters lifted the stretcher and walked away. Their only protection was the white cuff with the red cross. I admired their courage. In all the armies of the world, medics and their assistants risked their own lives to save the lives of their comrades.

The medic crawled out of the hole and Zerbi crawled back in. "Everything else okay with you?"

We nodded.

"I have to go."

He hurried to the nearest, frantically waving compatriots.

We lay under cover for quite a while, keeping our heads down. The enemy had us pinned down. We could neither advance nor retreat. I was afraid it would drag on into the night. Time became surreal. A thousand thoughts went through my head. I couldn't estimate how long we would hold out, when suddenly the humming and buzzing increased and finally the sound of aircraft engines was drowned out. Our eyes darted upward. Shadows hovered above us.

"Stukas!" shouted Zerbi, pointing upwards.

"Finally," groaned Lieutenant Huebner.

"Hurraaaaa!" came from all sides.

The first squad had identified the positions of the Russian grenade launchers and attacked them. Bombs were released.

Boom!

Explosions followed one after another.

This is the gate to hell!

Another group of Stukas swooped down and attacked Russian positions and Soviet-occupied houses. The wail of the sirens made your blood run cold. The guns were fired.

Tak tak tak

Muzzle flashes, roaring engines, wailing sirens, detonations and the constant rattling of the ship's guns woke us from our fearful lethargy.

Immediately, the Soviet shelling subsided. I breathed a sigh of relief. I even dared to raise my head and risk a look over the top.

Lieutenant Huebner checked the magazine of his submachine gun, then jumped up. "Attaaaack!"

From the tangle of stones, rubble, and debris, the Landser rose and stormed off with a loud "Hurraaaaaaa!

A second wave of infantry came running up from behind, supported by several assault rifles. We were literally swept away.

Man becomes machine in battle. Rash reactions. Survival is the ultimate goal. Humanity no longer exists. The soldiers mutate into merciless, slaughtering beings.

I also left my cover, opened my mouth and shouted at the top of my lungs: "Hurraaaaaaa!"

But the enemy was not defeated. They still fought back. The barrels of their guns rose as if from graves, muzzle flashes betraying their positions. The return fire struck like an iron fist, tearing life after life from our ranks. But there was no turning back for us. We went forward.

"Hurraaaaaaa!!!"

The first Landser reached the hall. Hand grenades were hurled. Muffled detonations were followed by screams, yells, and whimpering.

I put one foot in front of the other and stayed close to Zerbi, who ran ahead of me. By the time we reached the factory, the first of our comrades had already entered the huge building.

45

Lieutenant Huebner waited until we had grown to about two groups. Then he raised his right hand, pointed ahead, and shouted to drown out the noise of the battle: "We have to get to the end of the building and get inside! Follow me!"

Kremer wiped drops of sweat from his face. He looked through the line and was relieved to see that our group was complete. "Ready!" he signaled.

"Forward!"

Bending over, we hurried along the wall of the building. Our group was at the back, I was the second last.

Patch

One of the men running directly behind our platoon leader fell to the ground, mortally wounded. The man behind him stopped, bent down, shook his head briefly, tore off his badge and got back in line.

Patch

As soon as he was back in line, he also fell to the ground. He had been hit in the kidney area. The scream of pain was the worst and shrillest I had heard since my frontline missions.

"Ahhhh ..."

Two men immediately tended to the wounded man.

Bandages

One of them fell backwards with a blow to the head. The other threw himself to the ground. His scream sent a shiver of fear down our spines: "Sniper!"

Lieutenant Huebner ran on with the front section, while Sergeant Kremer raised his hand and immediately yelled: "Full cover!

"Miller!" Kremer yelled. "Miller, damn it, find that son of a bitch and shoot him!"

Patch - Zing

After Kremer shouted this sentence at me, he made a small sideways movement. It saved his life. The Russian sniper's bullet grazed the soldier's steel helmet. Pale as a sheet, the head soldier crouched behind a pile of rubble.

I tried to track the angle of the shot, but I couldn't make it out. My thoughts circled around the sniper like a merry-go-round.

He couldn't be behind us, because that's where our own positions were. He couldn't be hiding straight ahead or in the factory building. No way!

46

It remained a manageable radius. When I raised my head briefly to get an overview, three of my comrades shouted at me: "Get down!"

I immediately pulled my head back down.

My God, how careless. I must concentrate better!

A group of engineers ran along the wall. The men were trying to catch up with Lieutenant Huebner.

They were led by an older sergeant. When I spotted them, I started waving wildly and yelling: "Look out! Sniper!"

Patch

The sergeant grabbed his chest and stopped immediately.

I turned my head and slid up to look over the rocks.

Patch

Without looking, I knew that the second shot had meant certain death for the sergeant. But it also showed me the Russian's position. I had spotted him.

Now you're mine, I thought.

The hunting instinct, coupled with a lot of anger in my stomach, had taken hold of me.

Don't be overconfident, I urged myself. My position was not good. I retreated a little and crawled away, flat on the ground, over rubble and stones to the side. The Russian was lying in the middle of a large pile of rubble about a hundred meters from us. He must have entered from the side away from us, because the muzzle flash was visible in the middle of the rubble.

The engineers were in the same panic as we were. Lieutenant Huebner, however, had reacted, and the machine gunners with him fired a few rounds into the debris field. This gave the sap-pers time to get their bearings.

"Move up!" whined Huebner in the meantime.

"Bloody Stalingrad," Kremer grumbled, pulling himself up. The expression in his eyes changed to one of determination. He clutched his submachine gun so tightly you could see the white of his knuckles. "Men, forward!"

None of the Landsers moved. The machine gun still rattled.

"Miller! You get that Russian! Everyone else after me. Jump up! March, march!"

Kremer jumped up and ran off. My comrades stood up like marionettes and followed our squad leader. The engineers also got up and ran off.

I took aim and swept the barrel of the Russian sniper rifle across the stones in front of me. The stock of the Mosin Nagant felt cold against my cheek at first. The noise of the battle around me seemed to be drowned out. Everything faded away. My mind was focused solely on the Russian sniper. I looked through the scope. Since I had only ever shot without a scope, this was a new experience for me. Suddenly everything was within my grasp. I looked for the spot where I had seen the muzzle flash. The pile of rubble was an ideal place to hide. If I hadn't remembered the long iron wire sticking out with a piece of cloth flapping at the end, I probably wouldn't have been able to find the spot.

One meter to the left, then half a meter up.

I had it. I could see a small hole in the spot. Maybe 50 x 50 cm in size. It reminded me of an embrasure in a fortress. The machine gun volleys were fired at regular intervals. At one point, the trail of bullets flying into the rubble came very close to the hole.

I waited patiently.

Why is he taking a break? Has he retreated? Has it become too dangerous for him? Does he need to reload?

Maybe it was only seconds. Probably not even a quarter of a minute, but it seemed like an eternity.

You're hunting a human, Alfred. Can you do it?

I shook the thoughts out of my head. I thought of a cold beer, a fair, and good music. It worked. The doubts about my plan vanished.

My right forefinger was on the trigger and had reached the pressure point. My breathing was shallow. The rifle rested. I couldn't delay the shot. I felt my pulse, every heartbeat, and my knees became weak. Meanwhile, my hands were surprisingly steady, my vision clear, my resolve firm and unwavering.

The barrel of the rifle, pushed through the opening, was wrapped in cloth and difficult to see. Despite the telescopic sight, the head of the Russian sniper was only dimly visible. I didn't hesitate for a second. He was practiced, and it would take him only seconds to acquire a target, pull the trigger, and hit it.

I inhaled and held my breath for a moment as I exhaled. I was on target and squeezed the trigger. Even before I felt the recoil on my shoulder, the Russian's gun barrel tilted forward and came to rest.

I hit him! I hit him!

I could hardly believe it. I had killed the Russian who had shot four, five, six of my comrades.

48

I took a deep breath and waited for an inner stupor, but it didn't come. It was just the opposite. I felt slightly euphoric instead of depressed. I stayed there for a while, then I crawled back, got up a few meters away and ran to my comrades who were about to enter the factory building.

Kremer nodded to me as I pressed myself against the brick wall next to him, panting, and reported: "I got him!"

"Miller, you're a hell of a guy. We're going to need you and your gun a lot more in this nest. Take care of yourself!"

He had meant it. He had actually called me a son of a gun. I was full of pride at that moment and felt like a winner for a few seconds. It wasn't until the next command that I returned to the real world.

"Move up!"

We entered the factory building. The sight inside shocked me. In the huge hall that led into other rooms, nothing was in order. The ceiling had partially collapsed. Everything resembled a field of rubble, just like outside on the forecourt. Steel and iron rods protruded from chunks of concrete. Machines and thick strands of cable were crushed into undefinable tangles. Lieutenant Huebner lay behind a large, turbine-like steel structure and fired. There was a flash at the muzzle of his submachine gun. Cartridge cases were ejected from the weapon.

Kremer climbed over a fallen comrade, raised the barrel of his submachine gun with a small movement, and fired in the same direction. I couldn't see a thing, so I stayed close behind Zerbi and finally took cover behind one of the machines.

Huebner had emptied the magazine, ducked down and slid a new clip into his weapon. Ricochets whistled around. One entered Weinberger's left cheek, pierced it, and came out the right side. Within seconds, his face and uniform were covered in blood. The private recoiled in shock. Shocked, he dropped his carbine and grabbed his cheeks with both hands. He felt the warm blood and looked at the red smeared palms of his hands. At the same time, he began to whimper softly. Two comrades who were lying next to Weinberger immediately took care of him. One talked to him while the other nervously pressed a handkerchief to one of his cheeks. The paramedic was called. Hectic, loud and almost helpless.

"Saniii ... Sani ... tääääter!"

Pling - Zing

49

Again and again stray bullets flew through the factory hall and whirled around us. One of the two helpers was grazed in the shoulder. He looked at the small wound, pale as chalk.

I still held the sniper rifle in my hands, but I was unable to act. An eerie fear paralyzed me, held me in its grip. Whether it was seconds or minutes, I didn't know. My ability to react returned only when Zerbi tapped me on the shoulder and shouted: "Ivan's up and ahead. We're not getting anywhere. One of the Pioneers crawled over to us at the same time. "Where is the lieutenant? We have to get out of here! The Ivan is too strong. We can't move a meter from here!"

Hand grenades exploded. The noise was hellish. Dust, small pieces of stone and shrapnel swirled around. The shock wave was crushingly close. I instinctively turned sideways to protect myself.

"Forward! Up you go!" shouted Lieutenant Hübner.

When I turned around, the Engineer was lying in front of Zerbi, covered in blood. He had been badly mauled by shrapnel. The young soldier's gaze was broken, his eyes staring into space, his face ashen.

"Get the Russians who are up there!" Zerbi shouted at me, jumped up and hurried to Lieutenant Huebner.

I searched for the enemy, breathing shallowly. Muzzle flashes and small clouds of smoke revealed at least two Red Army soldiers. I took aim, aimed and fired. Repeating and re-aiming was one process. I was on target. I took a deep breath. The index finger moved slightly backward, the pressure point was overcome. The shot broke, the butt striking my shoulder.

"Now!" I heard the powerful voice of our platoon leader.

The men stood up and ran for the nearest cover. Two or three fell to the ground and were immediately hit again. The noise of the fighting grew louder. Three Red Army soldiers suddenly rushed out of a side room and fired into the backs of my comrades. I shot one of them. While I was still shooting, the other two Russians were in hand-to-hand combat with the advancing compatriots. One of the Russians went down instantly. The other fired from the hip with his PPSch 41 submachine gun. Two German soldiers were hit before a sapper shot the Russian in the back and then cracked his skull with the butt of his carbine. I swallowed and closed my eyes. The cold of the war had gripped us. No one was immune. If for a tenth of a second I was still wondering where the Engineer got the freezing cold to crack a man's skull, it immediately occurred to me that I had killed at least four, five, or six people in the last 24 hours. I detached myself from the wall, stood up, and yelled: "Hurraaaaaaa!"

I screamed my fear at the top of my lungs and stormed off. With all my strength and as fast as I could, I wanted to reach the new cover. I stubbornly looked up, searching for Red Army soldiers. Then it happened. Everything happened in a flash. I caught my right leg on an iron bar, stumbled and fell. Clutching the sniper rifle tightly, I couldn't break my fall with my hands. I slammed my head and face into the crankshaft of a wrecked machine. The wave of pain from the impact instantly enveloped me in darkness. I felt as if my skull had been split open. Then I was gone, unconscious.

Someone slapped my cheeks. I opened my eyes. Everything was blurred. The noise of battle raged.

"He's alive!" we heard.

I tried to sit up. Everything was spinning. I felt sick. I spat.

"Get him out!"

They grabbed me and put me on a stretcher. I must have tried to resist because one of the helpers said: "Stay calm!"

A deeper voice said: "Give him a morphine pill!"

I tried to reach for the Mosin Nagant.

"No, I think he wants the gun!"

"Give it to him and get out!"

They put the sniper rifle on the stretcher with me. I picked it up and clung to it as if it were a life preserver on which my life depended after a shipwreck. Off they went. The wobbling and shaking on the stretcher hurt. There seemed to be blacksmiths in my head, beating faster and faster with their heavy hammers against my brain. Everything throbbed. I closed my eyes. A relieving darkness surrounded me.

As the bearers left the factory, I heard the tracks of the tanks. The giants pushed over the piles of rubble and fired their guns. The Russians responded with volleys from the barrels of their dug-in guns.

Rumble

Near us, one of the tanks had rolled over a mine and broken down. It was immediately hit by a gun.

Rumble

Fate struck. A direct hit tore the steel colossus apart. Shrapnel and sharp-edged pieces of metal flew explosively, forcing the two medics carrying me to take cover. I fell off the stretcher, hitting the ground and screaming in pain as my head hit hard again.

There were crashes and bangs everywhere. Flames shot into the sky. The screams of the wounded mingled more and more with the "Hurrah" of the German soldiers, who were defending themselves against the counterattack and the "Urähhh" of the Red Army soldiers. Weapons rattled, bayonets flashed. Bodies collided. Hard steel burrowed into soft skin. Pistols and sharpened shovels shattered bones. Fierce hand-to-hand combat raged.

"Keep going, keep going!"

The medic's voice sounded duller than before. I was still clutching the sniper rifle. I didn't want to let go. It was like my life depended on it. When they put me back on the stretcher, I finally lost consciousness.

The battle for the factories in northern Stalingrad was fought with extreme ferocity by both sides. The losses were enormous. On the one hand, the commander-in-chief of the German troops, General Friedrich Paulus, was under enormous pressure from the Führer's Headquarters, which demanded the rapid capture of Stalingrad; on the other hand, the Russian commander-in-chief, General Vasily Ivanovich Chuikov, was under pressure from Joseph Stalin, who gave the order to hold the city at all costs.

Troops and materiel were constantly being transported across the Volga River to defend against the massive German attack.

The combat strength of entire divisions on both sides dropped at times to about 500 soldiers.

Soviet intelligence had learned that the main target of the German attack was the tractor factory and reacted accordingly. General Chuikov deployed his 84th Armored Brigade against the attacking German 14th Panzer Division.

The German troops met fierce resistance. Again and again Russian troops were overrun, crawling out of ruins, cellars or sewers and attacking the German superiority. Despite the fanatical fighting spirit of the Soviets, the tractor factory was almost completely taken by the second day of the offensive. German forces advanced to the Volga River.

The German air force flew non-stop supporting attacks on river crossings and resistance positions. The latter were vehemently expanded.

Narrow trenches were dug, caves were dug into the steep slopes of the Volga, and bunker-like rooms were built in the ruins.

The Red Army soldiers who landed at night had to step over hundreds of wounded comrades waiting to be transported back. The ships, boats and rafts were under constant fire from German machine gun nests and artillery. The casualty rate among the crews was correspondingly high.

But there was no going back. Political commissars mercilessly drove the Red Army soldiers into battle. Anyone who refused was immediately shot for cowardice.

For both sides, Stalingrad had gone from being a suburb of hell to hell itself.

A piercing headache brought me back to the real world. My vision was blurred. I tried to lift my head. Dizziness pushed me back into a pillow. Only slowly did I realize that I was lying in a bed. There was noise all around me. It smelled of carbolic and something undefinably disgusting. This unpleasant smell reminded me of a slaughterhouse.

Blood and decay, I thought.

I raised my hand and gently stroked my head. It was bandaged. Slowly the memory returned. We had entered that factory building. The fall. I tried to stand up again. This time it was a little better. I tried to get used to the dizziness. The piercing headache remained. There were several beds in the room. To my left was a man whose right arm had been amputated. Dried blood was visible on the bandage of the remaining stump. I instinctively moved my hands and feet, fingers and toes. I breathed a sigh of relief. Everything was still there.

"Are you awake?"

I turned my head to the right. Two beds away, a soldier was sitting on his bed. He was trying to get up with the help of two crutches. With a low moan, followed by a massive curse, he managed it.

"Ahhh, heavenly sacrament, for fuck's sake!"

The first two steps seemed a bit awkward and I was afraid he would fall.

"Ivan stabbed me in my left leg. The doctors here aren't bad. The staff doctor is a surgeon from Vienna. A great man. He saved my leg."

The soldier hobbled over to my bed and sat down on the edge. Then he held out his hand. "I am Franz."

"Alfred," I replied, extending my hand in greeting as well.

53

"You've been out for almost two days. You took quite a beating."

Before I could answer, an elderly nurse entered the room. "Hu-ber, you're walking again. You should only use the crutches to go to the bathroom and otherwise keep your leg still," she said in a sharp, unmistakable tone.

"I was just on my way. I was just introducing myself to this comrade."

"Well," she said curtly, then looked at me. "The young man is back with us as well. How are you feeling?"

"Not well," I replied in a slightly hoarse voice. Only now did I notice that my mouth was dry and my lips cracked.

"I'll bring you a cup of tea right away."

"Thank you. What ... uh ... what happened?" I asked.

"You narrowly missed a skull fracture. Your nose bone is broken and you have a massive concussion. We had to sew up a 10 centimeter laceration."

"How long will I have to stay here?"

"The doctor will decide. Rounds are in two hours."

Franz Huber got up again with a slight groan. This time, however, he refrained from cursing.

The nurse walked from bed to bed and then left the room. When Franz returned, he sat down by my bed again.

"It's not good to eat cherries with that sister. She's got hair on her teeth," he grinned. "But there's another one who looks really good. I hope I can go out with her someday."

"Where are my clothes?"

Franz looked at me in surprise. He was surprised that I didn't react to his conversation with the nurses.

"The guns are with the gunnery sergeant, the uniform should be under your bed."

"Did we take the factory?"

"You don't notice much here, but the artillery thunders incessantly. And the Stukas and Heinkel bombers fly every day. I can't tell you exactly."

"Where are we anyway?"

"Stupid question. In the field hospital. Here you get a break from the Ivan. The hospital trains roll out every day. I'm just waiting for the order from the senior field doctor and my certificate, then I'll say goodbye to this godforsaken nest."

54

I grabbed my head again. "This pain," I groaned. "I'm getting dizzy again."

The nurse returned and brought tea. I drank the cup almost in one go. "Do you have anything for my pain?" I asked.

She reached into her bag and handed me two pills. Then she poured more tea from a pot.

During the rounds, the doctor confirmed that I had a concussion. "You will stay here for observation this week and then do light duty for a week or two."

Time passed quickly. I became friends with Franz. By the third day, I was able to get up and walk around a bit. On the fifth day, Franz got the news that he was going home on the hospital train. A day later he packed his things and said goodbye to me. At that time, we didn't know what fate Franz would be spared. As he shook my hand goodbye, he said: "And when I come back after my recovery, Stalingrad will be ours and reconstruction will begin. What shall I bring you from home?"

I thought about it. "Maybe a little bottle of pumpkin seed oil. I miss it already."

"Typically Styrian," he laughed. "You'll get your pumpkin seed oil," he replied, limping away on his crutches.

I enjoyed the warm bed and the regular meals, but in the end, after that week in the field hospital, I was glad to be back with the troops.

I found it agonizing to listen to the moans of the wounded and depressing when another of my comrades was taken to the mortuary. Death had become a constant companion at the front, but you could never really make friends with it.

The east wind brought icy Siberian cold to Stalingrad. The first snow fell on October 22, 1942.

Harbingers of winter, I thought to myself as I slipped in the letter from the senior field surgeon. My uniform had been cleaned during my time in the hospital. After leaving my steel helmet at the factory, I left the hospital, which had been set up temporarily in a school, without a headgear and dressed too thinly for the weather. It was about ten kilometers to the battalion command post. I turned up the collar of my thin summer coat, put my hands in my pockets, covered my head, and waited.

55

My goal was to ride in one of the san-kas, or trucks, that brought in the wounded.

It wasn't long before a fairly young lance corporal joined me. He nodded, pulled a pack of cigarettes out of his field blouse, and offered me one.

"Thanks, I don't smoke," I declined.

Wordlessly, he took out a cigarette, lit it with his storm lighter, and put the pack and lighter back in his field blouse. A blue haze rose.

"Where are you going, comrade?"

I named my battalion.

"You're in luck. You can ride with us. I'll wait here for my taxi."

"Taxi?"

The lance corporal laughed. "My buddy Fritz. He chugs his Opel Blitz up to ten times a day from the airfield to the supply depot, from there to the hospital, and then back to the battalion. We agreed that he would take me with him on the next load."

"Great."

"You got it bad," he pointed at my face. The swelling on my nose had gone down quite a bit, the area under my eyes was rainbow colored. The fresh scar was covered with a large band-aid. "Splinter?" he asked.

"Something like that," I replied. I didn't think it was heroic to say that I was too stupid to run and fall while others were killed or injured by bullets and shrapnel.

"And you?" I asked curiously, since I couldn't see any bandages.

The lance corporal laughed. "I didn't take very good care of my rifle."

At first I was a little taken aback, but it quickly dawned on me what he meant, especially when he pointed to his crotch.

"One of the ladies infected me. Let me tell you, that treatment was hell. First they shoved something down my throat, then they gave me some really hot ointment. Believe me, comrade, I'd rather catch a bullet than go through that procedure again."

Now I began to laugh, too.

"Heinz," he introduced himself by name, and continued. "The worst thing was that it wasn't the doctor who did the treatment, but some kind of head nurse. Boy, was she anything but nice or squeamish. And she looked like she wanted revenge on all the wives who stayed home."

The next half hour flew by. Heinz was a gifted conversationalist. I couldn't say more than: "Hm ..." or "Yes ...".

56

The hum of a truck engine could be heard. The Opel Blitz came slowly around the corner and stopped right in front of us. The driver waved.

"That's it, I'll ask if you can come along for a ride."

Of course I got a ride. While Heinz sat in the cab, I squeezed into the back. The truck started slowly. My eyes fell on the buildings in the little village. Small, bright houses. Most of them thatched, surrounded by gardens and fruit trees. The picture contrasted with the ruins of Stalingrad, just a few kilometers away, with its brick buildings and once rumbling factories.

The land was vast, cold, and dirty. The rain had softened the soil. The east wind was piercingly cold, the sky gray and cloudy. I was shivering, but I was glad to have a vehicle.

During the ten kilometers to the battalion command post, we had to stop twice. Once assault rifles rolled by and once we had to let oncoming ambulances pass.

As my thoughts turned to home, images of my parents flashed through my mind. In two months, Dad would go out and get a Christmas tree. I closed my eyes and could literally smell the aroma of freshly baked cookies. Vanilla crescents. Mom baked mountains of them.

The rumble of the guns grew louder and inevitably brought me back to the sad reality. At one point the driver stopped and rolled down the window. "You'll have to get off, comrade. There's a field police post around the next bend. I don't want the chain dog giving me a hard time for picking someone up and losing the column, so to speak," he shouted at me.

"All right, and thanks for the ride."

"You're welcome."

I jumped off the bed. The truck started and drove off. I followed the road and a few minutes later I actually came upon a military post. Two field gendarmes were standing at an intersection talking.

Their tin signs shine even in cloudy weather, I thought.

Next to their bicycle with sidecar was a veritable forest of signs. I walked straight up to them and greeted them politely, then began to look for the right way through the maze of signs and warnings. The larger of the two chain dogs, a sergeant with sunken cheeks, spoke to me in the first tone and with an almost sinister expression.

"Where are you going and where did you come from? Let's see your pay book!"

I pulled the pay book out of my blouse and at the same time the letter from the senior field doctor and handed it to him. "I need to go to the battalion office."

The sergeant took the papers and checked them. He asked a little more kindly, "Did you walk all the way?"

"Yes, Sergeant," I replied briskly.

"Well, don't be so formal," he said in a rather relaxed tone. "You have to go this way," he points to the right. "It's not far now. Go past the first few houses, then turn left into a side street and go straight."

He handed me the papers, nodded, and resumed his conversation with the other gendarme.

A good fifteen minutes later, I was standing outside the battalion office. A dispatcher ran past me, jumped on his DKW NZ 350, started the engine and sped off. Two bucket trucks drove down the street. The hum of the engines above me made me look up. A fighter plane was returning from a mission. One of the planes had a slightly dark tail.

Hopefully the pilot will make it, I thought to myself, entered the building, immediately pulled the letter from the senior field doctor out of my blouse and reported to the battalion command post.

The room was pleasantly warm. In one corner a fire crackled in a kind of cannon stove. In the middle of the room was a large table with a map spread out on it. Front lines were drawn on it. To the right was a desk where an elderly sergeant sat surrounded by a mountain of papers. To the left and right of him were many files. Next to the small window was another table with a typewriter on it.

"Another one of limited use. Dirty, miserable one," the old clerk growled as he read my escort invoice.

Despite the severity of the sergeant major, there was something kind in his eyes. He reminded me of my boss in the Reich Labor Service.

"We already have two sick men here. Where would you be best employed? Perhaps as a dispatcher ..." he thought and finally asked: "Have you learned anything?"

The task of the battalion command post was usually to relay incoming and outgoing orders to the front or to neighboring forces, to process situation maps, to prepare situation reports for the regiment, and things like that. I had been wondering for some time why I had been sent here.

"What do you mean?"

"Am I not speaking clearly? My God, that blow to your head must have destroyed more brains than they thought at the hospital," the old soldier grumbled, looking at the plaster on my head.

"No, I understood everything. I'm a journeyman locksmith."

"Locksmith. Hm..." he thought. "Miller, Alfred ...", it seemed as if something had clicked in his head. "Miller, Alfred," he repeated. "There was something. Wait a minute!"

The first sergeant got up and walked out of the office. I waited more than ten minutes. When he returned, he was carrying a tray. On it were two cups and a pot of steaming coffee.

"Why are you standing there? Sit down!"

Confused, I sat down on the wooden chair in front of his desk. The first sergeant put down the tray, filled both cups, and sat down. Then he fumbled in one of the drawers and pulled out a green bottle. He opened it with a grin: "The finest Cog-nac! I won it playing cards. I don't want to know how my comrade got it, but I don't care. Here..." he said and poured a big gulp into each of the coffee cups.

"We ordered you here because your company commander knows our boss here very well. Captain Staller is also known as the Aide to the Deputy Commander."

I nodded. "Yes, that's clear, but you don't have any use for me, do you?"

"Not here in the battalion command post, but we've heard from your company that you're an excellent marksman and that you're sui-table as a sniper. Captain Staller actually wanted to talk to you in person, but things are crazy out there. He and Major Brenner had to join the regiment."

I took a sip of coffee and tasted the strength of the cognac. It felt good. Hot and strong, it flowed down my throat and warmed me twice over. A pleasant taste spread over my palate. I immediately took another sip. "Delicious!"

The sergeant drank as well, put the cup down and said: "This is real coffee, not crap. You can taste it right away, and that little brown one..." he pointed to the bottle of cognac, "...is the good kind, too."

General questions about me followed. It wasn't clear to me if the sergeant had to ask these questions or if he was just curious and wanted to pass the time.

Ring ... ring

The shrill sound of the field telephone, reminiscent of grinding gears, interrupted him. He picked up the bakelite receiver and answered with his unit and name. Then he jotted down a few sentences, nodded and mumbled: "Yes ... yes, I'll tell the captain."

I emptied my cup. In passing, I noticed that the sergeant had turned pale. The euphoric serenity he had exuded when I first appeared in his office seemed to have completely vanished. He put the phone down on the fork, picked up the bottle of cognac, and poured a generous amount into his cup. Without being asked, he poured some for me as well.

"If you want coffee with it, help yourself. I need the stuff straight for now."

"What happened?"

He put the cup to his lips, drank it all in one go, and looked at me. "We're going to make ourselves at home here, Comrade Miller. We'll settle in and get everything ready for the winter. The front lines will be supported by Hiwis. Dig trenches, build bunkers. The horses are collected and will spend the winter in the stage. It's supposed to be easier for supplies. They say they'll just stand around and eat anyway."

I shrugged.

"That means no advance, Miller. No advance and no retreat. The artillery and a lot of other units can't move without horses. We're holed up in this nest."

"But if we knock out the Ivan and Stalingrad is ours, then ..."

The sergeant major interrupted me. "Stalingrad is a ruin. There are no shops or markets for shopping. It's as cold at the end of October as it is at home in December."

I was speechless. What he said was absolutely true.

"Well, then I'll just apply for a vacation over Christmas," he added, topping off the bottle again and letting the bottle of cognac disappear back into the drawer with the remark: "One more sip will do."

We toasted, drank, and were silent for a while.

"Sniper," I said, breaking the silence. "You brought it up earlier."

Even though the first sergeant was on a first-name basis with me, I kept it formal. I didn't want to offend him.

60

"Do you smoke?" he asked, pulling a pipe and tobacco from his jacket pocket.

"No."

He stuffed the tobacco into the bowl of the pipe and pressed it firmly with one finger. "I smoke a pipe every afternoon. Preferably after my coffee."

Preparing the pipe was a real celebration.

"Do you play Shuffleboard?"

"Yes," I nodded.

A benevolent grin appeared on the sergeant's face. He put the pipe in his mouth and murmured. "You can call me Gustl. And if you have time, we'll meet soon to play cards. I already know who else I'll invite."

The sound of engines. A look out of the window. The first sergeant puts his pipe aside. "The old man's coming back. I think he wants to talk to you personally."

"Me?" I asked, confused.

"Think very carefully what you do," he warned me.

Footsteps in the hallway. The door was opened. As the Captain entered the room, I jumped up and clicked my heels together. But before I could greet him, the officer waved me off and said casually: "Thank you, no report."

I was a little nervous and excited.

"Is this the man?" he asked the first sergeant.

"Yes, sir."

The captain's eyes fell on the two cups. "Cold outside. Any coffee left? I could use something hot right now. Something twice as hot," he winked at the old soldier. "You know what I mean. Bring it to my office."

"Yes, Captain."

I had to wait another half hour, then Captain Staller saw me.

"You have been reported to me as an excellent marksman. Your pla-toon leader also mentions in his report that you took out two Russian snipers. You also successfully covered an attack. We can use men like you."

Staller paused for a moment and took a sip of coffee. He grinned. "I'm usually very strict about alcohol on duty, but sometimes you have to let things go."

The captain was likable. Even though he seemed so relaxed, he still exuded authority. He reminded me of my principal. He glanced over the

61

doctor's letter. "Well, Miller, if you like, I'd like to use you as a sniper. The Russians seem to have a lot of them in this nest. They're starting to do a lot of damage. Do you think you're up to the task of being a sniper?"

I cleared my throat. "Well, I haven't really thought about it."

"As a sniper, you will be taken out of your squad and report directly to your company commander. Although ..." the captain took another sheet of paper and read it, "... a lot has happened in the last week. Your company commander has fallen seriously ill. Apparently he has dysentery. Your platoon leader, Lieutenant Huebner, is taking over his position after the platoon was almost completely wiped out in the fighting in the industrial district."

I was startled, "Excuse me? Do you know what happened to my comrades?"

The captain shook his head. "I don't know the casualty list, Mil-ler. The fact is that the attack has stalled. Enemy snipers are having a massive impact on our supply and reporting routes. We must act now. Can I count on you?"

"You mean I'll be back with Lieutenant Huebner?"

"Yes, that's what I said. As a sniper you are under the command of your company commander. In consultation with the regimental commander, I would send you to our regimental weapons master. There, you will have the opportunity to test weapons, do target practice, and prepare for your mission. I would even give you one more week. Please let me know what equipment you need. We will make sure you get everything you need."

I didn't know what to say and hesitated. Images flashed through my mind. The house-to-house fighting, the storming of the factory, the artillery fire. I didn't want to go through that again. I thought at that moment that as a sniper I would be my own boss. I would be the hunter and not the hunted. It wasn't true, but that's what made me agree to it. Nodding, I said: "I am ready for the task and would like to try it."

The regimental armourer was a small, odd-looking fellow with nickel spectacles. As I entered the old smithy where he kept most of his arsenal, he was filing away at a piece of metal pipe. He wore a leather apron over his uniform, which was much too big for him. It probably belonged to the village blacksmith in whose workshop the sergeant had taken up residence. Without introducing myself, I heard his falsetto voice: "The old man has given you carte blanche as far as equipment is

62

concerned. Either you're related to him, or he's afraid of you, or you're really good at what you do."

"I, uh..." I stammered.

"Close the door. There's a draft!"

I complied with the request.

"Come here, boy!"

"You should have my rifle. I had it..."

"The Mosin Nagant with the 3.5x scope?"

"Yes, exactly."

"I did a little work on the rifle. It was in lousy shape. I had to replace the bolt handle. The scope is good. These PU models are great stuff anyway. State of the art.

I was glad the rifle was here. Somehow I saw it as a kind of good luck charm. "Thank you for that."

The sergeant put down the file, took off his nickel-plated glasses and cleaned the lenses with a handkerchief. Then he put them back on. "You have an observer?"

"Observer?" I repeated.

"Son, you know good sharpshooters always work in pairs."

"But the captain didn't say anything about that."

"Dilettantes! All dilettantes," he scolded, walking around the workbench, bending down, grabbing something, and holding my rifle in his hand. "Here's the good one. I shot it at 100 meters."

He put the gun on the workbench, bent down again and picked up a box.

"Here I have a few hundred rounds. All from the Ivan. I'll also give you some binoculars and a compass. And a pistol. Do you know what happens to snipers who fall into the hands of the enemy?"

"They kill them, don't they?"

The sergeant laughed out loud. "Kill? Yes, my young friend. You will die, but miserably. They'll torture you to death. I know stories you don't want to hear, because otherwise you won't be able to sleep."

The Oddball's look had changed. His eyes narrowed and he stared at me. "If you're lucky, they'll just cut off your index finger and shove it up your ass. If you're unlucky, they'll shove the barrel of the gun in after you and let you die laughing. If it's cold, they'll light a fire on your chest and warm themselves with it."

"These are horror stories!"

"Look at it however you want. Just be warned and think carefully whether you want to send another Russian to hell with your last bullet or allow yourself a quick death."

I swallowed. My Adam's apple was moving up and down.

"How did you even get the idea to sign up as a sniper?"

I cleared my throat and began to speak. I told them about Wagner and trying to get water. Then about the attack on the factory. "And finally I said yes."

"I'll put together some equipment for you. Then you'll have a chance to break in your gun. After this week, you will be able to load, aim, pull the trigger, shoot, disassemble, clean, and reassemble it by heart in your sleep. I promise you that!"

"You know a lot about sniping."

The sergeant didn't react to my remark. He turned around, went to the other end of the smithy, opened a large chest and rummaged through it. He closed the lid and muttered: "Where did I put that?" He thought for a moment, scratched the back of his head, and snapped his fingers. "I know now. Wait here!"

"Of course," I said.

The sergeant left the forge. A cold wind blew into the workshop from outside. I looked around, then picked up my rifle and examined it. It was shiny.

Oiled!

I put one hand on the bolt handle and fired. Unlike the first time I captured and used the rifle, it was much easier to handle.

It's amazing what this man has done with the rifle.

The sergeant came back. "Make room on the table over there," he huffed, and kicked the door a little awkwardly, causing it to slam shut behind him.

I put the sniper rifle aside and walked over to the table. There I pushed aside some uniform parts, wooden sticks, cardboard boxes and targets. The weapons master slammed his pack down on the table.

"You're going to need this," he gasped and unrolled the ball. There were four sheepskins sewn together. Then he placed an 08 pistol, a holster and two magazines, each holding eight rounds, and a combat dagger on the skin.

"This used to be mine."

"You ... uh ... you used to be a sniper?"

64

"The you is all right. We're on the front line here, not in the barracks yard. And to answer your question, no, I wasn't a sniper, but I trained a few. In theory and on the range, I've got it all down."

"You know about guns. The Mosin Nagant shoots a lot better than it used to."

He laughed. "I'm a trained gunsmith. If there's one thing I know about, it's weapons," the weapons master replied, raising his eyebrows. "By the way, our regimental commander has always had a soft spot for sharpshooters. He is a veteran of the Second World War and was first introduced to snipers in France. The old man likes to use them one by one. Here," he said, handing me the 08. "It will penetrate a steel helmet at ten meters. It's a good gun. Do you know how to use it?"

"I think so."

"Hm ... I'll probably pack a few more rounds for you to practice with. If you draw the gun, you should hit it. Practice makes perfect," he said, holding the dagger out to me next.

Meanwhile, I strapped on the pistol and loaded the magazines. Then I took the combat dagger, pulled it out of its sheath and weighed it in my hand.

"A bayonet is too long. This one is practical and most of all, really sharp. I made it myself. You can cut paper with it. I hope you won't have to, but sometimes you may have no choice but to kill quietly. You can either slit Ivan's throat or stab him in the kidney area. It depends on whether you want to kill silently or inflict enormous pain on your opponent. The latter may be part of the tactic. They won't leave a screaming comrade lying there carelessly and will help him instead of chasing you".

"Tactics? That sounds rather cruel."

Without answering my comment, he continued. "You will need tactics from time to time, my friend. You'll learn a lot in the next few days. Only if you take everything to heart in the field will you have a good chance of surviving out there, in that damned nest called Stalingrad."

I felt a little sick to my stomach. I had signed up to be a sniper because I thought a few shots at close range would be fine and I would be protecting the lives of many of my comrades, but I was worried about what the weapons master was telling me. He pointed to the sheepskin.

"You will lie warm on it or it will warm you from above. It's been freezing for days. It's going to snow soon, and the Russian winter is anything but our friend. When you're a sniper, you're often exposed to the elements. Believe me, you'll be grateful for this coat.

I tapped it a little awkwardly, as if I wanted to check it, nodded and rolled up the fur. Meanwhile, Franz put something else down for me. "I have here the most important utensil for the weapon. The Russians use a special gun oil in the winter. They also cover their bolt locks with special protective covers. I don't have much of this stuff, but you can have it, of course."

"Thank you very much."

"Have you moved into your quarters yet?"

"No, but I'm supposed to stay here with the regiment for the next few days.

"Our blacksmith has gone to the stage with the horses that have been removed. His sleeping place is free. You can stay here and save yourself the trouble of going to and from the stage when we're practicing our marksmanship."

"But there are still some horses here."

"He'll be back. But as long as he's not here, you have a good place to stay."

A stone fell from my heart. The weapons master was sympathetic and I was aware that I could learn a lot from him.

"Here, next to the forge, is his chamber. The fire in the forge also warms the back of the wall," he grinned. "You'll be nice and warm there. Besides, it's not far from here to the field kitchen."

"With pleasure. I'm Alfred," I held out my hand to the eccentric weapons master.

"Franz."

The room assigned to me was no larger than ten square meters and must have been the journeyman's dwelling in the past. The furnishings were extremely sparse. A bed with a straw sack, a small, clumsy table, a wooden stool, and two hooks on the wall for clothes. On the table was a burning candle. Next to it were matches. There was no stove in the room, but Franz was right. The wall the bed was against was the back of the stove and therefore warm. The journeyman's room had probably been added at some point.

I slept very restlessly that night, but not because of the difference between the bed in the hospital and this simple place to sleep. The restlessness was caused by what lay ahead. The life of a sniper seemed to be much more complicated than I had expected. It was only when I thought of my unhappy love at home and the storming of the factory that I calmed down and fell back into this emotional lethargy.

It couldn't be worse.

After a breakfast of commissary bread, butter, jam and hot coffee, the shooting exercises began behind the forge.

It was below freezing at night, and the air was still uncomfortably cold in the morning. There was a mist in front of our mouths.

We were still wearing our summer coats, and after a short time the cold crept under the thin fabric.

"It's our turn this afternoon. The winter clothes will be issued," Franz said casually. He had two empty ammunition boxes with him and counted the steps as he walked away from me. He put one box down at exactly 100 paces, the other at 150. He came back, grabbed a few more items and walked back to the two boxes. He placed a target on the front of each one. On his way back, cursing loudly, he used a hammer to pound five wooden posts, each about a meter long, into the slightly frozen ground at different intervals. He placed something on the smooth top of each pole and fixed it in place. When Franz came back to me, he simply said: "After five shots, the gun will be warm. You will shoot the front box five times. Then reload, do twenty push-ups, and fire at the second box. Also five times. Then you're going to jump up, run around the smithy, and when you get back here, you're going to shoot at the cans I put on the posts.

"All right."

He handed me five single rounds and two loaders with five rounds each. "Use the two clips first! I don't care how you shoot. Fire at will!"

I loaded the gun, knelt down, took aim and fired five shots at the first target. I reloaded and did the required twenty pushups. I lay down on the floor for the follow-up shots. I felt the cold and realized my first mistake. I hadn't brought the sheepskin and was annoyed about it. I was a little out of breath and it took me longer for the first three shots. I also lacked my usual accuracy. After the last shot, I jumped up and ran. I circled the forge, lay down on the floor again, gasped, dug the first round out of my pocket and maneuvered it into the chamber. I took aim, wobbled too much and fired anyway.

Next to it! Shit, it went right through me.

Nervously, I reloaded the gun, took my time, fired the next round and hit the target.

The third bullet went into the chamber. While I was aiming, Franz threw a stone next to my gun. Startled, I missed the shot.

"Come on! They're coming at you!" Franz shouted and hit my button just as I was about to reload.

The fourth bullet fell out of my hand.

"React or you're dead!"

I jumped up angrily. "Damn, I thought I was doing target practice!"

"You just got shot. You've blown your cover!"

I took a deep breath. "What was I supposed to do?"

"When the enemy is too close, you have a weapon. You have to fire and retreat. You can only fire one shot at a time from one position, because Russian snipers might be lurking across from you, just waiting for your second shot to send you to hell! Unlike us, the Soviets have entire sniper battalions at their disposal. And believe me, my friend, they know their business. They also have many female snipers in their ranks. If you ever come face to face with one, don't show her any mercy. Otherwise, she will kill you. Never forget my words!"

We inspected the hits. Franz was very pleased. "Apart from your misses, they're all within the range of a Schoka-Kola can. You're really good, Alfred. Now we'll shoot a few more rounds with the rifle, then we'll switch to the pistol. After lunch we go over to the temporary clothing store. The winter uniforms have arrived. Tomorrow they will be issued to the troops. Today it's our turn."

With each round I became more familiar with the weapon. Franz had also tied the cans to the posts with a string. After the can was shot off the post, it would swing back and forth on the string. My job was to hit this moving target a second time. The second can moved a little further back with each pass. The longest distance was about six hundred meters. Franz had placed an old steel helmet on top of the box and I had to hit it. When I had done this exercise twice in a row, we went to dinner.

As soon as we got near the field kitchen, the smell of goulash was fantastic. We were early. There were only three Landsers ahead of us.

"Potatoes on the side. Delicious!" I said, suddenly feeling how hungry I was. First I got a portion of potatoes in the pot, then the kitchen bull ladled goulash over it.

"Hans, give the boy a good man's portion. I'll give him a good beating this week," Franz said to the man standing behind the field kitchen.

He nodded silently, dipped the ladle back into the cauldron, and filled my cooking utensils to the brim.

"Enjoy it!"

It tasted delicious.

Later, when we picked up our winter uniforms, Franz used the same phrase again. He seemed to know everyone personally, and everyone complied with the armorer's request without objection. By the afternoon, I had not only received the winter reversible jacket and pants, but also thick gloves, a woolly hat, woollen socks, and most importantly, the coveted felt boots, which not all of my comrades had.

"Snipers are not popular everywhere, Alfred. You're always welcome wherever the Russians are. But when you sit as a sniper by the warmth of your comrades' stoves, the conversations may fall silent."

"Why?"

"Men from all walks of life serve here. Very few of them volunteer. They would rather be at home with their families or girlfriends. They are ordinary people. Soldiers who have never harmed anyone until yesterday, and tomorrow will go into hand-to-hand combat with a sharpened spade to split the skull of a young Russian. They fight to survive. They see you as a cold-blooded ..."

"Murderer? No, Franz. I'm not a murderer, because I only kill the Russians because they kill our people. Any one of the Russian snipers, man or woman, would shoot dozens of our men if I didn't finish him off."

"That's exactly what you have to tell them when you feel disgust."

I began to think.

"Stop thinking about it, Alfred. It's no use. War is not heroic. It's dirty, cold and mean. Only those who are faster, think dirtier and are colder than the enemy will return home.

Armsmaster's words echoed through my head, eating away at my brain like an ulcer. I had taken not only the first, but the second and third steps toward becoming a sniper. I was going to see it through. I was going to be my own boss. I no longer wanted to lie in cover and jump up on command to run forward amidst Russian grenades and machine gun fire. I wanted to be the silent hunter. I wanted to stalk and eliminate the Russians who wanted to do the same to our people.

Over the next few days I got to know my weapons very well. As in my training with the K 98, I was able to blindly disassemble and reassemble the sniper rifle and the 08.

Alfred brought me a kerosene lamp for my chamber. "So you can see better when you clean the weapons," he had said.

On the fifth day of my little training, a bucket truck pulled up. I was just about to cut some pieces out of a bed sheet to wrap around my gun for camouflage. The driver stopped. An officer got out, rolled up the collar of his coat, slammed the door and went into the smithy. Now the driver got out, stood next to the bucket truck and lit a cigarette. It wasn't long before the officer and Franz came out of the smithy and walked straight toward me. I recognized Lieutenant Huebner, stood up and saluted as he stood in front of me.

"Miller, let me have a look at you," he said, looking at my scar.

"I took off the cast yesterday and the stitches will come out tomorrow."

"Looks good again."

"Thanks," I replied.

"Captain Staller gave me a free hand. I am glad you have decided to be available to us as a sniper. How long do you think it will be before you're ready for action?"

Franz rushed to answer. "As far as shooting skills go, the boy is fabulous. But I'd have to give him a few more days of training in camouflage and tactics."

Huebner thought for a moment, looked at my wound again and finally said: "If you don't mind, I'll see you at company headquarters in exactly one week."

I saluted. "At your command, Lieutenant."

Huebner returned the salute and turned to leave.

"May I ask a question?"

He stopped and turned back to me. "Please."

"How are my comrades?"

"The combat strength of the entire company is down to 50 men. I lost half my platoon in the fighting at the factory. Of your group, Sergeant Kremer, the indestructible Corporal Zerberich and young Hofer are still fit for action. Weinberger went to the military hospital with a bullet hole in his cheek."

Half the platoon flashed through my mind.

"Thanks for the information."

Huebner nodded and went back to the bucket truck.

Franz tapped me on the shoulder. "We have a few days left. We want to use them. Camouflage will be the next topic."

70

Over the next week, the weapons master taught me how to blend into my surroundings. With his help, I assembled a few essential items. In addition to the sheepskin, these included a folding spade, a white sheet, an old blanket, a net to which various things could be attached, and two empty tin cans. He gave these to me on the last day of training.

"What am I supposed to do with this?" I asked in surprise as he held the cans out to me.

"You have learned to camouflage and hide well these past few days. You know you have to blend in with your surroundings."

"Yes ... so? What does that have to do with the cans?"

"You will be both hunter and hunted. Sometimes it can take days before you get the shot. At least if you're hunting a specific target."

"You showed me that I should create several hiding places and leave each one by a predetermined escape route. You drilled into me that I only had one shot, and then I had to leave the hideout immediately or remain silent. A second shot could betray me. I risk my life with every exception."

Franz nodded, but he remained silent and didn't say what I needed the empty cans for. I racked my brain.

What had I missed? What did he show me?

It didn't occur to me. Finally I asked directly. "Please tell me!"

The Master-at-Arms grinned. His eyes rolled a little behind his nickel glasses before I heard the sergeant's falsetto voice. "Just think, you've done everything right. You have a perfect position. You know for a fact that the Russian sniper who has already killed dozens of our comrades is going to visit his hideout in the next few hours. You're lying right across from him, waiting for him. But then, while you're stalking each other, your butt pinches or your bladder squeezes. You can either wet your pants, which will quickly become uncomfortable as winter sets in, or use the cans for the necessary business. But you still have to be careful. Your fresh poop will vaporize when it's cold. So put snow over it immediately or otherwise make sure that no clouds of steam are visible."

I was amazed. They had thought of everything, but not urination. "Franz, you're a real sniper instructor. You really think of everything."

"I'm just trying to eliminate the things that could end your life as avoidable mistakes."

71

It had grown cold. When Adolf Hitler gave his speech in the Löwenbräukeller in Munich, Franz and I sat in front of the radio outside the city limits of Stalingrad and listened intently. We drank hot tea and vodka. Franz had organized the bottle, as he called it.

Excerpts from the speech prompted comment, first from the armourer, then from me. We were drunk and alone. No one could prosecute us for our cheeky or critical remarks and drag us before a military tribunal for what we had said. We gradually became involved in the matter.

The unmistakable voice of the leader was captivating, the statements were infuriating. Despite the constant crackling of the radio, everything was clear and easy to understand.

"So if Stalin expected us to attack in the middle ..."

"We, when I hear that," Franz grumbled. "I didn't see our leader fighting next to me, did you?"

I shook my head.

"... I wanted to come to the Volga, to a certain place, to a certain city. Coincidentally, it bears the name of Stalin himself ..."

"Then why don't you come here?"

"Franz, not so loud. If anyone hears us, you'll be locked up for draft evasion," I warned.

The armourer just made a dismissive gesture with his hand. I laughed.

"There are only a few small squares left. Now the others say: "Then why don't you fight?" Because I don't want another Verdun, but because I prefer to do it with very small shock troops. Time doesn't matter at all. No more ships will come up the Volga, that's the decisive factor!"

I remembered the battles in the workers' district. I remembered the artillery attacks of the Russians. I thought of my fallen comrades and clenched my fists. "A few small places. We're supposed to hide here, and at home they're sitting in the pub, drinking beer and ordering roast pork!"

To loud applause, Franz poured a refill. Then he turned off the radio. "Cheers, my friend. Tomorrow you report to the company. I hope you've learned enough to survive."

I raised my cup. "To you, Franz. Thanks for everything you've taught me."

That night, icy winds had brought a bone-chilling, deadly frost to the dying city. The thermometer dropped to minus 18 degrees. Winter

72

had extended its cold fist to us. Even the wide Volga began to freeze. Ice floes made shipping, so important to the Soviets, virtually impossible. German artillery was largely concentrated on the passages of the river that were still navigable. Any attempt to cross the Volga was a suicide mission.

To keep the enemy under constant pressure, German troops attacked the Russian defenses on a daily basis. The Soviets were never to rest on their laurels.

The next major German attack was scheduled for November 11, 1942. The severely depleted divisions formed battle groups. The goal was to capture the last pockets of Soviet resistance and push the Red Army across the Volga for good.

The 100th Panzer Division was also assigned to this attack.

Despite the good winter clothing, the cold crept under my uniform. I was glad when I finally reached the company command post on November 9, 1942. It was in ruins. Pioneers had boarded up a shell-scarred wall with wood and put in a few support beams to hold up the ceiling. I knocked but didn't wait for an answer and entered the room. A pleasant warmth emanated from a crackling fire in the cannon stove.

Sergeant Maracek and our sergeant major, Wohlleben, were busy with paperwork. The clacking of typewriter keys stopped as I stood in the doorway.

"Miller! Come in," the skewer said, standing up. "Close the door. It's freezing in here. It's draughty in here anyway."

Maracek scratched his back. "Those damn lice. Yesterday I got twenty of them before I fell asleep! I really have to go back to the doctor and get deloused."

"It's no use. Those things are everywhere," Wohlleben commented. "Miller, the old man is waiting for you. You can go right in and see him."

"Why don't you give him some hot coffee first," Maracek interjected. "The guy's frozen through."

"Thanks, that would be really good."

"You can leave your stuff here," Wohlleben said, pointing to my rifle and the backpack where I had stowed all my gear.

"That's fine. I've learned to keep my gear with me at all times. I stick to that."

They both laughed.

"Come here, here's the coffee. But it's muckefuck. Real coffee will probably not be served again until Christmas."

"The main thing is it's hot."

I took the cup and felt the warmth return to my body with the first sip. "Ah...nice!"

Ten minutes later, I found myself with Lieutenant Huebner. He offered me a chair and looked at me. I wanted to ask him what he was thinking, but I didn't dare.

"Snipers usually work with an observer."

"I've done exercises with the weapons master both with and without an observer."

"That's good, because I can't put a man at your side due to the tight personnel situation."

I was actually quite happy with this statement. I wanted to move through the ruins of the city on my own. I didn't want to have to consider anyone else, and if I did, I would only be putting myself in danger.

Questions followed about the short training and whether I was aware of the task ahead of me. When I had answered everything to the officer's satisfaction, he stood up.

"Come here," Huebner said.

On the wall was a map of Stalingrad. Various signs were marked with pencil and red and blue paint.

"This is where we are. Our task is to deceive the enemy about the scope and objective of the offensive with several targeted assault companies. Combat teams from the merged 305th and 389th Infantry Divisions and the 79th Infantry Division, deployed to the north of us, will clear pockets of resistance, including the Red October factory. The southern forces of the 295th and 71st Infantry Divisions will also be tasked with driving the Soviets out of their positions and across the Volga. The Ice Stream will then form the new HKL for the time being. Our shock troops will attack here ...", he pointed with his index finger at some points on the map, "... here and here. I want you to go to the HKL today and observe. Maybe you can find out something. For example, if and where Russian snipers are stationed. You will report back here at noon on November 11. When we go into battle, you will eventually accompany the troops and provide flank cover. Just do what you did last time. Now go to the field kitchen. I've left a written order with the company sergeant. You will be issued cold rations for two days."

74

I nodded wordlessly. This was my first official mission as a company sniper. I was pretty excited, but I didn't want to show it.

"Do you have any questions?"

"Should I also shoot...", I searched for the right word, "...?", I added.

"Every dead Russian sniper will no longer be able to shoot one of our comrades. Every dead Russian officer will no longer give orders, and every dead Red Army soldier will no longer carry out orders, Miller. Do you have any further questions?"

I shook my head. "No."

"Dismissed!"

I left the room and reported to Wohlleben and Maracek. The latter was already holding up the letter from Lieutenant Huebner. "Here you are, Alfred. This is your food package."

"Cold food at sub-zero temperatures. That doesn't sound very comfortable," the Spit growled and rummaged around in his drawer. "There it is," he finally said, pulling out a bottle of juniper brandy. "Open your canteen. We'll pour you the still warm coffee and some of this. I'm sure you'll need it."

I smiled, thought of Gustl and his cognac, and wondered if all the soldiers in the typing pool kept a bottle of schnapps in their drawers.

"Thank you. Tell me, where do Zerbi and the others live? Do you think I could pay them a visit?"

Maracek grinned. "On the way to the field kitchen. There's nothing wrong with a quick visit. I'm sure they'd be delighted. Tomorrow they have to go back to the front. The rest period for our bunch will be over then."

"I just heard from the boss. We're attacking again."

I took the letter for the kitchen bull and put it in my pocket. Meanwhile, Wohlleben filled my canteen. "But I won't put too much of that stuff in, you're still supposed to aim and hit," he laughed.

Maracek saw how little juniper schnapps the skewer poured into the canteen. "Say, the bottle is half empty anyway. Give it to the boy. Who knows...",

"That's okay," Wohlleben waved me off and put the bottle of schnapps next to my canteen. "Take this thing with you."

After the route was explained to me, I said goodbye.

"The food carriers will also meet at the field kitchen. You will go with them to the factory grounds. Then you can drive a short distance. The rest you'll have to walk," Maracek told me.

Outside the door, the cold hit me in the face again. I shouldered my rifle and started walking. Desolate streets. Rubble. Few people to be seen. Mostly soldiers. Here and there, hooded children begging for food. But I also saw women of all ages trying to make themselves look reasonably pretty in order to prostitute themselves to German soldiers in exchange for food. Small signs, a wave, a quick smile, were used to initiate a relationship.

In the background, artillery fire from both sides never stopped. The rumble of the guns was as much a part of Stalingrad as the never-ending black smoke or the rotations of the planes of both sides, taking turns in their attacks. I was glad that the attacks were far away from here and began to hate the war more and more.

What kind of inhuman world is this?

A group of Landsers marched past me. Their unshaven faces looked tired and worn. Those who wore scarves pulled them up to their noses. The collars of their coats were all turned up.

The summer uniform immediately caught my eye.

They looked at me as I passed. Their eyes kept lingering on my Mosin Nagant, causing them to whisper. They also stared enviously at my felt boots and warm, padded winter jacket. At first I nodded in greeting, but when there was no response, I averted my eyes and walked on in silence.

I recognized Zerbi from a distance. The lance corporal's walk was inimitable. He carried a bundle on his back. I accelerated and quickly caught up. He turned and climbed over a pile of rubble, cursing as he stumbled over an iron bar sticking out of a concrete block and almost fell on the other side of the pile. "Crucifix, God forbid...damn...again!"

He let go of the bundle to keep his balance. Wood rolled over the debris.

"Watch where you're going. Some people ended up in a military hospital and have a pretty scar on their face for life," I shouted at him, reached the small pile of rubble, climbed up and pointed to my still shimmering red scar.

Zerbi immediately started to laugh. "Ha ... ha ... Alfred, you young Styrian bull. Nice to see you again. Come on, help me gather the wood. It's getting scarce in Stalingrad."

A few minutes later we were standing in the bunker of Sergeant Kremer's group. Bunker was probably a bit of an exaggeration. The house the men lived in was, of course, in ruins. A few Hindenburg lamps and a large candle provided light. A small workshop stove gave off a pleasant warmth. A little smoke from the stovepipe kept the billowing out.

They didn't get it quite right.

So it smelled a little smoky. But it was warm.

The reception was very warm. I didn't know any of the men except Hofer, Kremer and Zerberich. I was quickly introduced.

"Servus."

"Hello."

"Griaß di," was all I heard. No one bothered to get up. I unbuckled my rucksack and put the rifle down beside me. Then I sat down and put the bottle of schnapps on the clunky table.

"What have you got there?"

The place came alive in an instant. Even the new comrades, who seemed lethargic at first, sat up or came straight to the table. "Juniper schnapps!"

"Golly, Miller. It's like Christmas has come early."

"Give us your cups. We'll share."

In less than a minute, there were eight cups on the table.

"This fits like a glove. After the next offensive, I'm going on home leave," Kremer grinned. "Then Zerbi will be your squad leader for a while."

"Since when do you know that?" the old corporal asked, reaching for the bottle, nodding at me and pouring about the same amount of schnapps into each cup.

"Since yesterday, when I picked up the field post. The spit told me. And he slipped me something else."

"Like what?"

"When I return, you will be gone."

Zerberich lifted the cup, drank it all at once, slammed it down on the table, and filled it again. "Me?" he asked, his voice almost shaking.

"I don't know any other Lance Corporal Zerberich."

"Christmas at home. I never thought of that."

"After Kohler from the other group got it, you're the one who hasn't been home the longest of all. At least that's what the spit said."

"Raise your cups, comrades. We have a reason to celebrate!"

We clinked glasses.

"The first thing I'm going to do is get properly deloused. These beasts are driving me crazy," Kremer changed the subject, and each of the men had a lice story ready.

The goal was to see who could catch and crack the most lice each day. The record was held by one of the newcomers. "I caught 28 last night," he grinned. "Are you staying in the bunker with us? It'll be tight. We've already had to turn some away. Unfortunately, they don't have as comfortable accommodations as we do."

"I can't. I just wanted to say goodbye and see some old faces."

Kremer fell silent. The sergeant looked at my rifle. "Where are you going?"

"To the factory. I have to go to the field kitchen. I'll pick up rations there and go on with the food carriers."

"What are you doing there?"

"The old man told me we were attacking again. He told me to look around."

The lice recorder said: "What nonsense. What good is one sniper? If we attack the Russians again, the Stukas will bomb the Communists. Then ..."

Kremer interrupted him: "Soft bombs? Like last time? You know how many men we lost? Were you there?"

Silence.

"I... uh... no."

"Sepp, you should be quiet. You don't know what's coming," another of the new comrades reassured him. "You know, Sepp was at home. He got another five days special leave after his recovery because his wife had triplets."

"Congratulations," Zerbi said, lightening the slightly aggressive mood considerably.

"Recovery? Did you get it?" Kremer asked.

"Yes, but not the Russian, a truck. It was an accident. My leg was broken. Everything's all right now."

"So you weren't there for the first attack?"

Shake your head.

"Cheers. To your triplets. What are they?"

78

"A boy and two girls."

As the men began to talk about their children, I stood up and packed my things. "Got to get going. Don't want to miss the food carriers."

We shook hands.

"See you in hell," Zerbi groaned, raising his cup.

We sat in the back of an Opel Blitz. The cold was biting. The icy wind also carried individual snowflakes in front of us. I knew that winter was coming with a vengeance.

Just like back home in Austria when the weather changes, I thought.

"Damn city," grumbled an older sergeant. He held the large food container between his legs and kept staring at me.

"Stalingrad?" As soon as he said it, I scolded myself for making such a stupid remark. Of course he meant Stalingrad. What else could he mean?

"That's right! It should be called Stalingrad. Only ruins, only death! Do you know that in many of these ruins there are women and children? The poor bastards have nothing to eat and are dying under the bombs and shells, just like our comrades and the Red Army soldiers!"

"Be careful what you say, Paul," warned the man next to him.

"Why? What could happen to me? When we came here two months ago, there were ten of us left in our group. I'm the last one left. All dead or in the hospital!"

"Paul is right! Our cemetery is getting bigger and bigger. The Russians seem to have a lot of supply divisions. And us? We're bleeding to death!"

"They can't hold out much longer. You'll see."

I decided not to get involved in this discussion. But I thought it was the same everywhere. Everyone was grumbling and unhappy. Suddenly the truck lurched. I instinctively held on to my rifle so as not to damage the optics. The driver braked abruptly and the driver's door flew open. "Get out! Everybody out!" the driver yelled as he jumped out. "There's a sewing machine coming at us!"

There was immediate movement. Everyone jumped from the loading dock.

As night fell, the Russians used their slow biplanes, Polikar-pov Po-2s, actually known as U-2s. They were used for reconnaissance and ground attack. The pilots liked to drop bombs on worthwhile targets. We

79

called these aircraft, which were often seen very late, sewing machines because of their humming engines, or runway UvDs because of their permanent frontal control.

"Much too early. They usually come after dark. How can this slow thing fly over us unharmed?" the lead fighter cursed, ducking behind a pile of rubble next to me. The pilot turned around and seemed to be heading back to us when a machine gun rattled from somewhere. The tracer stretched into the sky. The sound of the engine faded.

We breathed a sigh of relief.

We waited another two or three minutes, then we heard the driver's voice again. "The Ivan has left. Get in the car. We're moving on!"

About twenty minutes later we finally had to sit down.

"From here we continue on foot."

Contrary to my initial fears, the snow clouds had disappeared.

It's probably snowing out in the steppe.

Despite the warm winter clothes, I shivered slightly and wrapped the scarf around my neck so that only my eyes looked out. The words I had heard on the journey were still echoing in my head. The sergeant had told me. The Russians had begun to use special tactics at night. In squads of up to ten men, armed with knives, spa-des, their PPSch submachine guns, which were reliable in the cold, and flamethrowers, they forced their way into houses occupied by German soldiers. Again and again they heard screams, then gunfire, and often flames from the ruins.

"One of the factory buildings," he said, "has four floors. We sit on the first floor, the Russians on top, then us again and Ivan on top. This Stalin tomb is crazy. The men have not only given the city a new name, but also the battle. It's no longer a war, certainly not a blitzkrieg, it's now called the Rat War! In Stalingrad we are fighting each other like rats."

The man at the front behaved cautiously. He oriented himself along a road, asked a Pak crew stationed there for directions, and finally waved us over.

"Our pile is still in the next street, just like yesterday. But our com-rades here think we should be careful. Ivan is active at night and always attacks with small raiding parties."

The sergeant immediately powdered his nose. "You see, just like I said. Rat war, damn it. They come to kill us quietly." He turned to me. "Comrade, I hope you're good with your rifle. Actually, I don't think much of you sharpshooters, but to be honest, I have to admit I'm glad you're coming with us."

At first I wanted to reply that this was my first sniper mission and that I was only supposed to do reconnaissance, but then I liked the aura the sergeant had given me and I nodded wordlessly.

Stalingrad was never quiet. Even now we could hear the clatter of machine-gun salvos. Artillery rumbled in the distance and the smell of gunpowder and burning was constantly in the air.

Pioneers had posted warning signs. Caution snipers! and Caution mines! could be read.

"Great! These black pioneers are funny. They plant their stick mines in the ruins and we're supposed to know where the stuff is," whispered the first man at the back.

"Just pay attention to the warnings. The comrades aren't that clumsy. They wouldn't foolishly mine our retreat areas," the sergeant reassured us. Apparently, the closer we got to the HKL, the more he mentally returned to his military skills and knowledge.

We arrived at our destination without incident. We were met by a sergeant. "You're the sniper," he greeted me.

Wondering how he knew that, I nodded. "Hunter Alfred Miller."

He waved. "Not so formal, comrade. Our reporter has announced your arrival. He wants us to brief you on the situation. However, I must disappoint you. You won't get much of a briefing. The situation is very simple. Here we are, over there the Russians. The area is nothing but a pile of rubble. Not a single house is intact. I hope our last day up here will be a quiet one. We'll leave the day after tomorrow and return to the stage to rest."

"Where are the Russian snipers positioned?" I asked, earning a dirty look.

"If we knew that, we would have smoked them out long ago."

"Actually, I meant..." I tried to improve my stupid question, "... if you've had any failures here due to Russian snipers?"

The sergeant thought for a moment. Not in my platoon, but two blocks away, they had two dead. That was this morning.

I made a note of that.

There was a faint bang in the distance. A machine gun rattled not far from us and a flare shot up.

"They're on the move again," the sergeant grumbled. "Where to with your food? We have to go back."

"Come with me."

81

A lamp burned in the ruins where the Sergeant had settled. A few men sat around it. They were wrapped in blankets. Bearded, expressionless faces stared at us. It was only when they saw the food containers that something resembling a smile flashed across their faces.

The sergeant sat down on an empty ammunition box, took out a pencil and a notepad, and took down both our situation and that of the Russians. As he was explaining, he tore the paper out of the pad and handed it to me. "...and if you have to retreat, watch out. The engineers have mined some of the houses. We'll surprise the Ivan when he tries to enter with his shock troops."

"How will I recognize these houses?"

"Not at all. But the engineers always mined the entrances and windows on the sides facing the Russians. They used only stick mines with wire traps. The backs of the houses are clear. So we could get in safely if necessary. There are exactly two of them. But we didn't occupy them. One is the building right next door, the other is further back... oh yes. There's a huge pile of rubble next to one of the houses with a streetlight sticking out of it. You can use that as a guide."

"We saw that. But there was a warning sign on the house."

"So they did mark it after all," the sergeant mused, only to add, "But hopefully not in Cyrillic." Laughing, he put his pencil and pad back in his pocket. "That's it, comrade. Good luck."

The sergeant looked at me. "Same time tomorrow?"

At first I didn't understand what the food carrier was trying to say and shrugged.

"You want to go back with us tomorrow?"

"Yes, of course. I'd get lost on my own."

"Same time then. We won't wait more than fifteen minutes."

"Thank you. See you tomorrow," I replied, looking at my watch to remember the time.

The food carriers left the ruins. It visibly filled with compatriots crawling out of their positions. Word spread quickly that there was food. One of the first had taken his portion, retreated to a corner, and lit his Esbit stove. "Finally something warm."

I thanked the sergeant for the information and left the ruins as well.

Outside, I took a quick look around, read the note again, and crouched down behind a few piles of rubble. An icy wind was still blowing, but I hardly felt it due to my excitement.

From the beginning, I had an idea that quickly turned into a plan. I wanted to go to the neighboring, mined ruin and take refuge there. I would feel somewhat safe there, and I hoped that the ruins weren't too decayed.

I need to get to the upper floors to get a good view. Then I need at least two positions in this ruin.

I reached the building. From the outside it seemed to meet my requirements. I almost made the mistake of entering the ruins from the side via a pile of rubble in front of a window.

Danger of mines, my head pounded, and I walked around the building. There was an open door in the back. I pulled out my flashlight, thought about whether I could turn it on safely, and looked around again. Feeling completely safe, I turned on the flashlight and shone it on the door frame.

No wire, no booby traps, I realized and entered the house.

Lights off! Pistol in hand.

Holding the .08 in my fist, I stayed away from the window and walked slowly along the wall. At the top of the stairs I turned on the light again. On the fifth step I spotted a wire. I stepped over it carefully and turned off the lamp.

I'll just stay on this floor today and inspect the ruins in the daylight tomorrow, I decided and looked for a good spot.

The temperature was somewhere between minus twelve and minus twenty degrees. An icy wind blew into the house through the broken windows. A piece of the front wall had been blown away. I crawled to it and carefully looked out. Satisfied, I began to set up my position. I quickly made a small wall out of a few stones. This would keep the wind out. I laid out the sheepskin, dragged a door to the wall I had built, and placed it over it so that it would look to an observer as if it had just happened to be there. Satisfied with my work, I crawled into the hiding place. Once I was comfortable, I took the rifle, aimed it, and looked through the scope at the streets and ruins of the city. I had a relatively clear view. I had long since gotten used to the sound of the artillery. It was a constant sound in Stalingrad. At this volume, however, it was bearable and okay for me. The shells fell far away. Both the trembling light of the flashes and the orange-red glow in the impact area painted an eerie picture in the night sky.

Often there were only a few steps between deadly icy cold and bla-zing hellish heat. But there was peace and tranquility here.

Was this the famous calm before the storm?

I pushed my thoughts aside and let my eyes wander over the ruins once more.

Very good, I thought, put the weapon aside, moved two more sto-nes in front of me to a different position and finished working on my first position.

My biggest problem will be the cold, I realized, took the woollen blanket from my backpack and wrapped myself in it. A feeling of free-dom enveloped me. I couldn't put my finger on it, I couldn't define it, but I was free from the usual chain of command. I was my own master. I could lie down and sleep whenever I wanted. I had a mission, but I wasn't under supervision. I was a hunter, likened to the privateers of the seas. Boarding and plundering for the crown. But also outlaws. If I fell into the hands of the enemy, there would be no mercy. It was a game of life and death. Me here, the Russian there.

Icy winds whistled through cracks, crevices, and gaping holes in the walls of the ruins. My little cave kept some of it out. So it was bearable. The sheepskin proved to be extremely useful, as it had been during the shooting exercises. It was comfortable, practical, and warm.

My parents' faces came to mind. I remembered how we decorated the Christmas tree and the smell of roast goose in my nose.

Christmas at home.

With this image in mind, I dozed off.

Rrrrrrt ... rrrt

Rumble

Machine gun fire and an explosion woke me from my sleep. Screams echoed between the ruined walls and mingled with the sound of gunfire. I was instantly wide awake. My muscles tensed as if electrified. Goose bumps spread over my body.

That's fear, boy, I realized immediately.

I didn't have to pretend or talk myself into anything. I felt real fear. I shivered, trying to convince myself it was the cold, but I knew it was the adrenaline my body was releasing to prepare for fight or flight.

The weapons master's words returned.

Your hypothalamus triggers the release of adrenaline when you are afraid or stressed. And as long as it doesn't become paralyzing fear, that's

84

a good thing. That way, you're always on guard and acting instinctively. Do you know what they do with the snipers they catch?

The answer to the weapons master's last question was probably responsible for my decision to die rather than be taken prisoner.

Take a deep breath!

I was alone. My stomach rebelled for a moment, my knees were still shaking.

Take a deep breath. Stay calm. You can do it! You can do it, I repeated quietly.

The shaking subsided. I reached for the binoculars, but I didn't need them to see what was happening in front of me.

Tongues of flame were shooting like a fireball from an upper floor of the building, diagonally opposite my position. According to the sergeant, it was not supposed to be occupied by our men. Since no explosives were detonated when the Soviets entered the ruins, I concluded that this house was not mined.

Damn it, where is the other mined house?

I saw two more men rush into the house. They were unmistakably Russians!

There was a long, shrill scream. Then a burning man jumped out of the window on the second floor. He hit the floor hard and rolled on it. The shrill roar faded to a soft whimper that I could no longer hear. My heart was pounding, my pulse was racing. I became angry and set the binoculars aside.

"You bastards," I spat, picking up the rifle and firing.

I watched the window and the front door, but saw no target.

Boom!

The explosion was booming. There were screams again, but also fragments of words in Russian. I panned one house over and saw through the optics that Red Army soldiers were also trying to get in. They were triggering one or more booby traps set by the sappers.

That's what you get!

Two Russians were dragging a struggling comrade behind them. One of them was limping.

Out of the corner of my eye I saw a movement. I turned back to the first ruin. Something was moving at the front door. I stayed on target. My index finger was on the trigger and had already reached the pressure point. A minimal movement would be enough to break the shot and send the bullet through the barrel. Milliseconds later, it would pierce the body of a Red Army soldier.

People ran out. I was about to pull the trigger when I realized they were civilians. Two or three women and four or five kids.

Damn it!

I was still breathing shallowly, still ready to shoot.

A flare shot up into the night sky, flickering and illuminating the scene with its artificial magnesium light. The man who had jumped out of the burning window lay still and motionless in the cold rubble. The women and children were sent in the direction of the Russian positions. One of the Red Army men urged them on, shouting loudly. Two small children began to cry.

"Dawei!" it came to me.

Only gradually did I realize that more of these small groups were on the move, scurrying through the rubble and entering the ruins.

Rrrrrrt ... rrrrt

The crew of a German machine gun position took advantage of the flickering magnesium light and fired a few rounds at the Red Army soldiers. They immediately took cover. The man with the flamethrower scurried back and disappeared into the entrance area of the ruins. The tracer ammunition showed the trajectory of the bullets like drawn lines.

Not bad, good shot, I thought to myself as I saw one of the Russians get hit.

The flare had burned up. Immediately, two of the Russian squads left their cover and stormed off. Their target was clear. It was the next house. The machine gun fired again. I also saw muzzle flashes on the windows of the building toward which the Red Army soldiers were running.

Boom!

The attackers had thrown hand grenades and managed to get the soldiers to take cover in the ruins for a short time. The Red Army soldier with the flamethrower worked his way slightly away from the others as they continued to force the Germans into cover with their machine guns. The second squad I had spotted was doing the same with the machine gun nest.

"They won't be grilling any of my comrades again," I breathed out, unloaded my weapon to load one of the Pr cartridges, and fired again. The process had only taken a few seconds. I was very familiar with the weapon thanks to all the training. I quickly found the flamethrower carrier again. He was already quite far away. I had him in my sights, aimed at the container of burning oil, and pulled the trigger. My phosphorus bullet was effective. The Red Army soldier exploded in flames. I immediately replaced the magazine strip.

Five normal bullets, I said to myself. Change position! You have to go now!

I wondered if anyone had seen the muzzle flash or if I could fire a second shot, contrary to what I had been taught.

Idiot! Pack up and get out of here!

I crawled out of my hiding place.

A wild firefight began in the street. The burning Red Army soldier gave off a macabre glow.

Rrrrt .... Rrrrt!

I hurried, rolled up my blanket and coat, strapped on my backpack and risked a last look at the street, when suddenly there was a loud rumbling on the first floor.

Droning

My ears were ringing. Screams could be heard. Screams of pain!

"Ahhh ... ahhhhh ..."

Droning

A second explosion brought certainty. I realized it with horror.

They are here! They're storming this ruin! Did they see the muzzle flash?

I thought feverishly about what to do. I fumbled nervously with the holster of my 08, finally got it open and pulled out the pistol. I was as quiet as a mouse, not daring to take a single step, but staying exactly where I was.

"Ahhh ..."

The wounded man screamed and whimpered violently. Full of fear, I waited for the tongue of fire from a flamethrower, but nothing happened. Instead, there was a babble of voices. A frantic exchange followed. The wailing grew louder. Voices again. The Russians seemed to be discussing what to do. Beads of sweat formed on my forehead. I wasn't kidding myself. I was anything but a stone-cold lone fighter. I wasn't a born hero, no Siegfried from the Nibelungen saga, I was a young man who felt pure fear of death.

I have to count when I shoot! The last bullet is for me! Damn it!

If I had inevitably become indifferent to life since the affair with my spurned love, I realized at that moment that I still loved it and wanted to continue living it.

I don't want to die!

The voices faded, as did the whimpering of the wounded man. The gunfire in the street had also died down. An eerie calm returned. While I waited, I made another decision. The Russians assumed that this ruin was unoccupied, otherwise they would have stormed the building and fumigated it. So I was safe, at least for the night. Where else would I go? After this action all sides were wide awake, our soldiers and the Russians. I would have to identify myself from a distance to avoid being shot by my own comrades. But if I did that, I ran the risk of being shot by the Russians. So I decided to stay. I went back to my position, unrolled my coat and wrapped myself in the blanket. I watched the road for a while. Only slowly did the fatigue return. My sleep in the second half of the night was very restless, but it was still good to rest.

It was broad daylight when I awoke. With every breath I took, a small cloud of mist wafted in front of my mouth. It was very cold. I shivered in spite of my winter clothes and warm blanket. As soon as I opened my eyes, I thought about the night's interlude.

So it wasn't a dream, I quickly realized.

I had fired my first shot as an official sniper, and I could sleep peacefully. I had no remorse. On the contrary. That Red Army man was about to send more of my comrades to the hell of flaming death. I beat him to it.

It was quiet outside. Except for the constant rumble of artillery from both sides, of course. I crawled out of hiding and stretched. After a few squats and some exercise, I felt a little warmer. At least the shivering was over. For the morning toilet I looked for a room I wouldn't use.

The temptation to make something hot with the Espit stove was great, but I didn't want to take any chances and decided to enjoy my breakfast cold, which I did.

Freshly fortified, I lay in wait again. I patiently watched the ruins and rubble alternately through binoculars and the sight of my rifle. The charred body of the German soldier was still lying on the pile of rubble where the burning soldier had fallen after jumping out of the window.

I spun around, looking for the spot where I had shot the flame-thrower man.

Everything was black and charred.

88

If the Russian I had shot was still lying in the black pile of burnt rubble, he was no longer recognizable as a human being. The war was cruel. I wondered how many sons, brothers, and husbands never came home. Why were we fighting here, so far from home?

As my thoughts continued to wander, something came to life. Two children emerged from one of the ruins. I was amazed and wondered if they were the same ones the Russian soldiers had chased out of the house that night.

No. Otherwise the women would be there, I told myself, watching them.

They could be brothers, I thought. One was a little taller than the other.

They moved deftly through the rubble, seemingly unafraid of the snipers. The smaller one spotted the burned German. He called his brother, and they both ran to the charred body. The boys knelt down. One of them held an iron bar or stick in his hand and tapped the corpse.

Son, he won't hurt you anymore. He's dead. My God, how hardened. I would probably have died a thousand deaths at that age if I had found a burnt man.

I watched them with fascination. Only gradually did I realize that they weren't testing to see if he was alive, but trying to feel him with that stick. They were searching for something edible or valuable. Now the big one had discovered that the Landser was probably lying on his haversack. He gave instructions to the little one, and they both grabbed the body to turn it over. This proved to be a difficult task. Either they were too disgusted to grab the man properly, or he was too heavy for them, or he was frozen to the ground.

"Come on ...", I was almost feverish. I wouldn't begrudge these poor devils a little success.

Now the torso was moving. They had actually managed to turn the body over. Through the binoculars I recognized the horribly disfigured face. I closed my eyes for a moment.

My God, you guys. How hardboiled are you?

They had indeed found what they were looking for and pulled a few things out of the burnt bag. The big one held something up proudly. I was convinced it was a can of fish and half a burnt commissary sandwich. The loot immediately disappeared under the big man's tattered coat, which was held together with patches.

Rrrrrrt

89

A machine gun burst into the rocks near the two boys and disappeared into the ruins behind them.

I was as frightened as the Russian children.

Is that machine-gunner crazy? What are you doing? Since when do we shoot at children, I thought. I was immediately furious. Only then did I realize that this was probably meant as a warning. The two boys immediately dropped to the ground, waited a moment, and when no more shots were fired, they jumped up and ran away. They disappeared back where they came from.

"Enjoy your meal! You've had your meal for today," I said happily to them.

Nothing moved until noon. Boredom set in. I also had to crawl out of my position again and again to warm up with gymnastics and stretching exercises or to get my circulation going again. After warming up my stiff body several times, I decided to eat something. Then I lay in wait again. In between, I wanted to go down and see what the Russians had done with the explosions they had set off.

To fight boredom, I memorized everything I saw in front of me. Road, rubble, ruins. I began to divide it into squares in my mind. Each one was like a picture, and I tried to remember everything I saw. I looked away and looked again. I looked for changes, for anomalies. I played the whole game for about an hour and a half to two hours, by which time I had memorized everything I could observe from my seat. Any change, I thought, would be noticed immediately.

Then came the shock. In the late afternoon, from one minute to the next, I felt like Robinson Crusoe who had discovered footprints on his desert island on the beach that were not his own.

In the middle of the pile of rubble lay a piece of corrugated iron, different from what I had remembered. A mixture of goosebumps, fear, excitement and self-doubt ran through me.

Calm down, Alfred! Think about it!

I tried to recapitulate and let the last 30 minutes pass in review.

I observed the area, then withdrew from the position inside the ruins and did my warm-up and gymnastic exercises. Then I ate and drank. All of my equipment was immediately packed up again, so that I only had to roll up my coat and blanket in case of a quick retreat. Then I took up my position again and observed the terrain almost with a certain routine.

With my imaginary map in mind, I started at the top left and worked my way down to the right.

No! That corrugated metal was definitely further to the right, closer to the pile of rubble with the window frame sticking out across it!

I was one hundred percent sure. I had memorized corrugated iron and window frames as fixed points.

Now it felt like a cold shiver of fear that sent goosebumps from the back of my neck to the soles of my feet. I immediately checked my rifle. It was loaded and ready. I quickly checked my watch. My heart started racing again, my pulse pounding. I placed it on the corrugated metal, stared through the scope, and waited. Over thirty minutes passed and nothing happened.

I'm not stupid! The thing wasn't here earlier, it was closer to the window frame, I began to doubt myself.

I wondered if I was going crazy, but I stayed on target. At some point I doubted myself and asked myself if I was imagining things with the sheet metal. I was on the verge of telling myself that it was all a figment of my imagination when suddenly I felt a movement. It was only slight. And I only noticed it because I was looking through the sights of my rifle at the exact moment when the front right corner of the corrugated metal suddenly lifted slightly.

Goosebumps and fear mixed with a kind of hunting instinct. A certain tension was palpable. My heartbeat and pulse continued to race. I put the rifle down and took out the binoculars.

Remembering the Master-at-Arms' words of warning, I made sure that no rays of sunlight or any other source of light would be reflected in the binoculars' glass.

Upon closer inspection of my target, I noticed that the corner of the corrugated metal sheet in question was supported by a small wooden stick. It was clear to me that someone was lying underneath. I immediately ruled out the two boys from the morning. They would never have acted so professionally and I would have noticed them long ago, so it had to be someone else. There weren't many possibilities. I suspected three things. A sniper, his observer, or an artillery observer. I quickly crossed the latter off my list. The field of view at this location was absolutely unsuitable for an artillery observer. That left a sniper and/or his observer.

I was glad I was lying down because my knees were soft. If I had put any weight on them, a slight tremor would not have gone unnoticed.

I took a few deep, calming breaths. Then I picked up the rifle and fired. The cold stock rested against my cheek.

What do you want here? Who are you? Shooter or observer?

As I aimed at the target, I became surprisingly calm. My mind was crystal clear. The breath of death always wafted through the streets and ruins of Stalingrad, but this time I felt it differently than before. I couldn't explain it, I had already shot it down, but this time it was like my first self-discovered lead. I had tracked down the wild animal, discovered it, and now I was lying in wait for it. Over there was a Red Army soldier whose goal was to kill my comrades. My task was to prevent that by eliminating this danger before he struck. It was this train of thought that gave me the strength to aim and shoot a Red Army soldier. I didn't see the person under the uniform, I saw the danger he posed. This difference did not make me doubt what I was doing. I didn't have a guilty conscience yet, and with this attitude I wouldn't get one. I didn't want to lose any more comrades. I didn't want the typing pool to have to pack up photos and a few belongings and send them to the bereaved with a letter of condolence. I wanted this war to end as soon as possible.

Stop thinking, I reminded myself. Concentrate on the goal!

For a moment I wondered if I should just fire a shot at the center of the corrugated metal. There was a good chance I would hit it. I estimated the sheet to be about 1.80 by two meters. A little smaller.

If I stop in the middle ... hm ... no! I'll wait!

I wanted to know who it was.

Shooter or observer?

I began to put myself in the place of my counterpart.

What do you want here? What is your goal?

After I tried to reconstruct the picture from the point of view of the Russian I assumed to be under the corrugated iron, there could be only one worthwhile target. The German machine-gun nest. It had stopped the flamethrower troops during the night and fought them off effectively.

It controls the road! That's what you want! You use a sniper to take out the machine gun nest!

Once I was sure of the target, I wondered if the sniper or the observer was down there. I quickly came to the conclusion that it had to be the observer. He would determine the trajectory of the shells or any movement on the German side and signal it to the gunner. So the gunner must have taken position within sight of the observer.

As a result of my theory, I now looked for a possible position on the Russian-occupied side of the ruins.

Nothing!

I definitely couldn't see anything.

They are not far away! You must see the signs of your observer.

If I waited for a shot, it would be a game of life and death. The price was high. The Russian snipers knew their business. This meant that if I let the Russian shoot just to see his position, it would mean the death of one of my comrades.

No, my friend! I will not pay that price. The breath of death will hit your observer. You will become blind and retreat. Or you will become angry and show yourself by making a mistake.

My mind was made up. The man under the corrugated iron was my target. I aimed at him. As soon as I detected any movement, I was going to pull the trigger. I had to be sure my shot would hit. I waited patiently.

Franz's face reappeared in my mind. I heard the sergeant's falsetto voice as he said, "Sometimes tactics require you not to kill, but to wound. You will take care of the wounded. Screaming and calling for help will paralyze them!"

The longer I concentrated on the target, the more I realized that I would never see this Russian. He had moved into position unnoticed and would disappear just as silently, unnoticed and invisible. He was hidden under the tin, at least from my position. As soon as he was successful, he would retreat.

I took a few more calming breaths. My decision had been made. Once it was dark, my chances would diminish, and the latent danger that the Russian sniper could strike at any moment worried me more and more. I didn't want to wait any longer and decided to take a shot. I imagined a man of average height, placed this mental image under the corrugated iron and aimed at a spot where I was most likely to get an effective body shot.

I assumed that the Soviets would not expect a German sniper to be positioned here.

Damn, it suddenly flashed through me.

It occurred to me that the shock troop from last night had noticed my shot and reported it. Then the Russian sniper wouldn't be after the machine gun, but after me. And this corrugated iron could be a trap to find out my position.

93

I breathed shallowly. I considered this second theory. Then I rejected it.

I have one shot, then I retreat.

I looked at my watch. It would be dawn in a good hour. My plan was set. I was going to wait until dusk, then shoot and clear my position.

Waiting was more nerve-wracking than I had first thought.

If the Russian actually fired before I shot the suspected observer, would I be responsible for the death of my comrade?

I couldn't stand it any longer and pressed the stock of the Mo-sin Nagant firmly against my cheek and shoulder. My index finger was almost clammy with cold, but I still had enough sensitivity to feel the pressure point on the trigger. I aimed at my target and squeezed the trigger.

The bang was terrifying. It shattered the unreal silence in my head, because in Stalingrad there was never any silence. You couldn't hear the birds singing, and the laughter of the people had long since ceased. Instead, you could constantly hear the rumble of artillery on both sides, detonations, or the echo of small exchanges of fire. No matter what sound reached your ears. In Stalingrad, it was death approaching.

But the one shot I had just fired sounded different to me. It seemed to catch among the rubble and ruins, returning several times as an echo. A weight fell from my shoulders as the bullet came out of the barrel. It was as if the flash of the muzzle had exploded the tension with its bright light. Everything happened in the same second. The shot cracked, I quickly drew back the gun and crawled backwards.

The bullet fired from my weapon pierced the thin corrugated metal, burrowed through the uniform and into the flesh of the Red Army soldier below, shredding his body, muscle tissue and organs before it was probably stopped by a bone and stuck deformed. A high-pitched scream followed and repeated itself as a continuous ordeal of some kind of pain release.

Hit, it fluttered through my head.

The certainty that I had been right was accompanied by the fear that there was a Russian sniper lurking out there whose primary target I had become with this shot. What would he do? After all, I had shot his observer and probably wounded him badly. At least that's what the shrill wailing suggested.

How did you react?

"Ahhh ..."

94

The cries of the wounded man grew louder. Cries for help, groans and whimpers. It all echoed in my head as I frantically rolled up my coat and blanket. I strapped on my backpack, shouldered my rifle, and pulled my pistol from its holster. Much as I was tempted to observe the situation through the binoculars, I decided against it. The Russian sniper would now be lurking with maximum concentration. Angry and with the desire to kill!

He would be searching the ruins with his binoculars.

He wanted me. That was as certain as the Amen in church.

He'll hunt me down. I shot his observer.

I had done what he had planned for us. I put fear into the ranks of his comrades, because they knew from that moment on that a German sniper was lurking in the ruins, waiting for them. Psychological warfare.

I cautiously approached the stairs, listened and took the first step. There was nothing to hear. The 08 lay in my fist, ready to fire. If any Russians had sneaked into the first floor unnoticed, I would sell my life as dearly as possible. I planted my foot on the next step and walked down the stairs in slow motion. My eyes were accustomed to the dim light, so I immediately recognized the fate that had befallen the Red Army soldiers during the night. There were splashes of blood everywhere, as well as larger and smaller pools of blood. Two mangled Russians lay on the ground. One had massive shrapnel wounds and was covered in blood. The other had half of his head blown off. Bone fragments mixed with brain matter clung to the opposite wall.

I swallowed and felt my Adam's apple move up and down. My mouth suddenly felt dry. I quickly climbed over the two bodies to get to the exit. I could still hear the constant screaming of the Red Army soldier who had been shot. He must be in terrible pain. The gun went back in the holster.

There was also a large pool of blood in front of the entrance to the ruins. It extended from the window here. I tried to reconstruct the events of the previous night in my mind. Judging by the blood, the injured man must have tried to enter the building through the window and was wounded by shrapnel from a booby trap. The other two entered the building from the rear and triggered the second booby trap. The two uninjured Soviet soldiers then rescued the wounded man and withdrew.

That must have been it.

I looked around and wondered if the Russian sniper could see my retreat. It was highly unlikely. Nevertheless, under the cover of the ruins, I moved slowly and carefully back to the sergeant's position, where I was to wait for the food bearers.

The voice of the first sentry was almost relieving. I had almost reached my goal.

"Stop! Who's that?"

"Hunter Miller! The sniper," I replied, instinctively ducking down a bit.

"All right! You can go on."

I climbed over one last pile of rubble, slid down the other side more than I walked, and finally reached the ruins of the Feldwebel.

While I was giving Lieutenant Huebner a full report the next day, the company was preparing for battle. I would never know if the Russian I had shot died or was saved by his men. There were no reports of sniper casualties. So the company commander thought the sniper had retreated and chalked up my first mission as a complete success.

The impending attack was aimed at the still stubbornly occupied Russian pockets of resistance. As with our 100th Panzer Division, new combat groups were formed in the 71st, 79th, 295th, 305th, and 389th Divisions from the men still fit for action. The major attack was prepared with air support. Four engineer battalions were added as reinforcements. Most of the engineers, however, were assigned to attack one of the main objectives, supporting the 305th Infantry Division in the capture of the Lazur Chemical Plant and the interlocking of the converging rail lines there.

Our task was to confuse the Soviets as to the actual objective and the planned scope of the attack by means of strong shock troops.

"...the task of the 305th Infantry Division is to completely liberate the Lazur and Red October factories from the enemy. We will distract the enemy and attack south of them. Our air force will wear down the enemy. Men, the Russians can't hold out much longer. We'll manage to drive them out of their positions tonight and send them across the Volga for good. You'll see, we'll celebrate Christmas in a Stalingrad liberated from the Russians!"

96

There was none of the usual rejoicing of the enthusiastic soldiers. The soldiers I joined looked haggard and tired. Some eyes stared into space, others were cold. Ice cold. And others showed pure fear.

Stalingrad is eating us from the inside, I thought at once.

The officer pointed to one of the houses marked with numbers. "An assembly point will be set up in house number 29. The intelligence squadron is ready and will set up wire connections between the company command posts as quickly as possible and also ensure that we are in constant contact with the battalion," he said and then paused for a moment. He looked around. "Men! The engineers are clearing the way for the infantry. Their attack is concentrated on the main Russian defensive position. We'll make it this time!"

As the sun set on November 11, 1942, the industrial district of Stalingrad glowed. The German Luftwaffe was preparing the attack that would destroy the last pockets of Russian resistance and drive the enemy out of the city, or at least across the Volga.

Under the fire of the enemy's anti-aircraft batteries, the fighters of the 8th Air Fleet attacked and bombed the predetermined targets. The sirens of the dive-bombing Ju-87s emphasized the horror scenario with their psychologically grueling howling. The detonations of the bombs and the defensive fire blended into an unforgettable infernal noise. After the explosions, bright flames shot up again and again. They were always followed by dark, dense clouds of smoke that hovered over the city like a veil of death, slowly descending on Stalingrad.

The Luftwaffe pilots scored some impressive hits. The towering factory smokestacks, which still rose like warning fingers from the rubble, were also hit and collapsed.

But the main objective, to bomb the enemy out of their positions, could not be realized. While factory chimneys and walls collapsed and buried many positions, while splinters and shrapnel whirled and bored into everything in their path, the long-suffering Red Army soldiers huddled in their holes and positions.

They knew that this killing spree by the German air force would be followed by an artillery attack and then an assault by tanks and infantry. In their more or less safe shelters or among the rubble of houses, factory buildings, railroad cars and holes in the ground, they waited for things to happen. Trembling and full of fear of death. Like all soldiers in the world, they thought of their families, of the things they loved. But they also thought of the enemy who had invaded their homeland, overrun it with fire and death, and whom they had to face so that their families could live.

They were bitter and cold. They hated. It was this hatred that gave them the strength and courage to face and fight the enemy. Hate was the driving force behind their actions.

The fair war the men had once been led to believe did not exist. It did not exist. And if it existed anywhere, it was not in Russia, and certainly not in Stalingrad. The only thing that counted here was survival. Man became an animal, a ravening beast. Everyone who fought here quickly learned that there was no danger from a dead enemy. So they had to kill. Kill to survive. No matter how!

The German compatriots, waiting in their starting positions for the end of the air raid and the accompanying attack signal, felt the same way. Nobody really wanted to be here. The fear of death was their constant companion. Empty, fearful and cold stares wherever they looked. Many of the men smoked without saying a word. Maybe it was their last cigarette. The cold crept under their coats. So the soldiers could blame their trembling knees on the freezing temperatures.

Some of the soldiers stared at photographs of their wives and children. Others were still shoving food into their mouths.

An older corporal sat next to me. He stared at me for a long time but didn't say anything. Finally, he reached into his coat pocket, pulled out a small package wrapped in newspaper, and opened it. A piece of salami and two slices of commissary bread appeared.

"If I'm going to die, at least I'll be full."

I nodded.

"Boy..." he said with an unmistakable Styrian accent, "... how old are you?"

"Nineteen!"

He bit into the salami, then the bread. He hadn't finished chewing when he asked the next question. "Doesn't that bother you?" he wanted to know, pointing at my rifle.

I wondered what to say, but a private with a long scar on his face answered for me.

"Do you have children?"

The private turned to his neighbor. "Yes. Two sons and a daughter. Why do you want to know?"

"Because our comrade with the scope will make sure your children don't lose their father. I feel safer when the snipers are on our side and not on the Russian side. I've already lost four of my comrades to the snipers!"

The corporal took another bite of salami, chewed a few times and swallowed. He looked at me and just said: "Then make sure I get back home."

Before I could answer, a green ball of light shot up.

"Forward! Get out of your positions! Aaaaan...griiiiiif!"

The remaining pieces of salami and bread were shoved into his mouth. A brief nod. Chewing, he stood up.

As if guided by a ghostly hand, my comrades stood up everywhere. An initially quiet "Hurray!" merged into one word. It was shouted from dozens of throats to get rid of the fear with the roar.

The attack signal had a releasing effect. Thought processes were switched off and replaced by soldierly automatism. They sprang to their feet, weapons ready to fire, senses sharpened, and ran toward the enemy. Hoping to avoid the enemy's defensive fire, they looked for the next opportunity to take cover as soon as they jumped up.

Two soldiers collapsed in front of and beside me. The urge to jump back down was enormous, but somehow I followed my comrades as they screamed in fear and tried to find their way through the wreckage.

Boom!

Grenades were thrown. Splinters, shrapnel and pieces of stone flew around. Again I saw one of my comrades fall. He had been hit by a machine gun bullet while running. Blood spurted from his neck and chest. The carbine fell from his hands as his legs carried him two more steps forward. He was dead before he hit the cold ground.

I knelt down. Bullets whizzed by close to my head. I frantically searched for something to crawl under. I spotted a large, half-standing concrete pedestal. I quickly crawled the few meters to it and found good cover.

Like an invisible fist, the machine gun kept punching gaps in the ranks of my comrades. I had to take it out.

Damn it! Keep your head up. You'll find it!

I peered over the cover. Just for a few seconds at first, then a little longer. Finally I saw the unmistakable muzzle flash of the machine gun. I slid the rifle over the concrete block and fired. In addition to the nervousness and fear, the heavy panting made my plan difficult. I tried to

99

calm down and took a few deep breaths. I feverishly searched for my targets through the scope.

There they were!

The machine gun nest and the gunners were well camouflaged, but the massive PM 1910 was clearly visible when firing. Two Red Army soldiers crouched behind the shield of the Maxim machine gun mounted on a wheeled cart.

Now it took me another minute, maybe two, to get my breathing under control enough to make good hits. By now I knew the importance of the exercises I had to do with the weapons master.

My chest was still rising and falling at breakneck speed. I knew I had to take out that machine gun right away. The attack on this flank seemed to be stalled by the power of this weapon. More and more Landser sought cover and had to be literally whipped forward.

Despite the twilight, there was enough light. I could see enough. I had long noticed the small movements behind the shield. I waited a moment, then I had enough control to take the shot. Part of a head appeared for a split second. I pulled the trigger, repeated it, and stayed on target.

A hit!

In a battle, I could not be recognized as a sniper, at least not too quickly. The machine-gun fire had stopped. I saw something.

Either an arm or a leg.

I pulled the trigger again. The shot cracked, the force of the recoil over the butt against my shoulder. I fired the repeater again. The machine gun still didn't fire. I had obviously gotten both shooters. One was a sure shot to the head, the other hit my arm or leg.

Unable to fight! Target reached!

The Landser stormed on. I jumped up and followed them.

Hand grenades whirled through the air, lowered their trajectory and detonated. We were in the railroad area, on one of the feeder lines to the big factories. A few railroad cars had been woven into the Red Army's defense chain. Shrapnel scratched the steel of the wheels or dug into the wood of the wagon walls. Gunfire flashed everywhere.

The distance to the first track was estimated at 50 meters. Several shell hits in a row forced us to take cover again.

I crouched down in a large crater. It was gradually filling with soldiers who were running through the enemy fire in search of cover. Among them were two engineers. I was glad to see them and hoped they were equipped with enough explosives to clear the way for us. The faces of the Landsers reflected fear and tension. The last men to squeeze into the funnel were a engineer and two rearguards. The pioneer had the rank of corporal. As soon as he came to rest, he shouted something to one of the radio operators. I only understood half of it because of the grenades going off at the same time. The radio operator nodded and fumbled with his backpack. While he was still trying to get through to the command post, we heard a noise that made our blood run cold. The rattling of chains and the roar of heavy diesel engines.

"Tanks!" went from mouth to mouth.

One of the pioneers tried to calm them down. "Don't be afraid, comrades. The drivers can't see anything in this twilight. They won't attack. I think they're moving into position to support the infantry men in the trenches with their firepower."

I believed him, for the constant fire that had finally forced us to take cover came from the tanks' guns and confirmed the engineer's words.

"What kind of trenches?" asked a young fighter.

"The Russians dug a small trench system behind the tracks. Our Stukas were supposed to bomb them out, but it looks like they didn't make it," came the deep voice of the other engineer. The voice matched his stature. He was about two meters tall and extremely strong.

"How can that be?"

"They probably had the tanks stored in one of the halls."

Questioning looks.

"Or they built some kind of bunker out of heavy railroad ties! What do I know? It doesn't matter how they did it. But as you can see, the tanks moved into position and ..."

Boom!

The impact of a grenade drowned out the rest of the answering sentence in the noise of the explosion. I felt the shock wave. A few small chunks of dirt and stone crashed onto my back. As soon as the nearby bang died down, a soldier not far from me called for a medic. Obviously he or one of his buddies had been hit.

I recognized medics plowing through the rubble to rescue wounded comrades, and I paid the highest respect to these Samaritans in combat.

How long will it be before they rush to the aid of the screaming soldier? Will they be able to save his life or that of his comrade?

The radio operator had finally reached the command post. However, the requested artillery support could not be provided. The barrels of our cannons were needed for the main target, the heart of the Russian defensive position. It was located in one of the halls of the Red October factory.

However, we received help when a group of grenade launchers moved in and fired on the trench and the tanks.

The explosions became more frequent again. This time, however, on the Russian side.

"Those are our boys," grumbled the tall engineer.

I noticed that his expression was more tense than before. The next thing I saw was that he was holding a T-mine in his left hand and a clenched charge in his right. The man's carbine was slung across his back.

"I'll stay with you and cover you," I said, receiving a silent nod. Somehow I thought I saw some relaxation in his face. But maybe I was wrong.

"Get out of the holes! Annnn...griiiiiiiffff!"

The voice of a headhunter pulled the men up. As if pulled by the strings of a puppeteer, they rose and charged the enemy again.

Rrrr!

Rrrrrrt ... rrrrrrtttt

We rushed forward. Shells rained down on both sides, tearing the men apart. Machine gun and rifle fire swelled into a huge battle roar. To the left, a ball of fire lit up the gruesome scene. The wind carried a few short cheers over the din of the battle. A T34 was burning after being hit by the grenade launcher unit.

Metre by metre we approached the trench system the So-viets had painstakingly dug behind the tracks. The first Landser jumped in. Close combat began. I saw one of the T-34's, its cannon firing shell after shell. The on-board machine gun was also blasting away, tearing holes in the ranks of our attackers.

A soldier running in front of us picked up a hand grenade, pulled the ripcord and hurled it forward. As it flew, the warhead spun around the handle. The grenade lowered its trajectory and landed in the ditch.

Bang!

Direct hit, it flashed through my head.

More and more Landser jumped into the trench. I saw two of them collapse just short of the trench, as if crushed by a huge, invisible fist.

When the third Landser fell and stayed down, I knelt down. Beyond the ditch were railroad cars.

Probably a siding.

I saw the muzzle flash of a rifle. A Red Army soldier had taken cover under one of the cars. He was a good shot.

Not a sniper, I realized at once. He would have looked for better cover, but he's still a good shot, I repeated in my mind and took aim. I took my bearings from the muzzle flash of his weapon. The remaining light was bright enough. My shot cracked. Sure that I had hit the target, I sped up and followed the burly pioneer. He had almost reached the ditch. Running ahead of him was the sergeant who had ordered us out of our positions. He stood in front of the trench, held his submachine gun to his hip, and fired several rounds into the trench. The sapper jumped in. I had caught up and jumped into the trench as well. I landed on something soft and was in danger of tipping over. Frightened, I looked down. I was standing on a dead Russian. Guts were spilling out of the torn abdominal wall. The face was unrecognizable, just a bloody, pulpy mass. I had to swallow. It was only the constant release of adrenaline coursing through my nerves that kept me from vomiting.

The trench was narrow. Very narrow. The sergeant, two soldiers and the engineer ran to the right. There were dead Red Army soldiers everywhere. One of the Russians was not dead, but wounded. He raised his arm for help, but instead of a helping hand, the soldiers ran over the man's body. Heavy knuckleballs pressed down on his chest, arms, and face. The burly sapper tried to jump over the Red Army soldier, but failed and landed on the injured man's chest. Ribs seemed to crack. The poor devil screamed.

Tormented man! Cursed war!

At that moment, I had to force myself not to stop, and continued to run after my comrades. The trench forked. While the sergeant continued to squeeze through the narrow passage, firing burst after burst from the MP, the engineer turned into a wider trench. It seemed to be an unfinished trench, because after a few meters we stood in front of a pile of dirt.

"Are we at the end of the trench?" the engineer gasped.

Despite the icy November cold, I was warm. Sweat clung to my uniform. A haze of breath hovered in front of our mouths. Suddenly, two Red Army soldiers appeared in front of us. They had climbed over the pile of earth and were running toward us. I immediately realized that we were not at the end of the trench, but that one of the aerial bombs had hit close by and had filled in the trench at this point.

The Russians were as stunned as we were. I immediately pointed the barrel of my rifle in their direction and fired a shot. I hit a Red Army soldier in the stomach. He ran two or three steps, then collapsed with a long, drawn-out scream on his lips and rolled on the ground in a heap. The second Russian jumped at the engineer. The latter shook himself like a bear trying to get rid of annoying bees after stealing delicious honeycombs. The Russian was thrown to the ground by the force of the pioneer. Then, with remarkable speed, the Russian dropped his concentrated load, reached to his side, and within seconds had his folding spade in his hand. Before the Red Army soldier could leap again toward the German soldier, the spade hurled downward. The blade struck his shoulder. Blood spurted, bones cracked. The Soviet soldier collapsed, screaming in pain. The sapper swung the spade forward like a side-sword blow and smashed the Russian's face, causing him to fall backward, mortally wounded and writhing bizarrely. Silently, the spade was strapped back onto the paddock. Without making a face, the pioneer picked up the clenched load and peered across the trench. "We made the right move. The T-34 is back there!"

I crawled over the mound of earth I had thought was the end of the trench and lay down flat. I could make out the outline of the tank. Behind and beside it, Red Army soldiers were firing. Muzzle flashes were everywhere.

More Landser came running up behind us.

I fired and killed two or three Russians. Then I put a new loading strip into the gun. Meanwhile, the sapper had left the trench and was crouching and running towards the T-34. We were diagonally behind the fighting colossus and I had to fire twice more at the Red Army soldiers.

"This guy is completely crazy!" I shouted and followed the engineer again.

I desperately searched for Russians who might attack us. In the meantime, however, I realized that we could now also come under fire from our own men.

"Damn it! The idiot has no brains!" I cursed.

I was terrified, but as if hypnotized, I ran after the peasant. Some of the Landsers who had joined us in the squadron followed us as well. They swarmed out. A flare was fired from somewhere and shot into the sky. Frightened, I lay down on the ground in the flickering magnesium light, took my rifle and looked for Russians. I shot at every enemy I saw.

The engineer had also continued to run in the bright light. He must have had tunnel vision and only had eyes for his target. The enemy tank!

I concentrated on the man and his surroundings. A face appeared behind the tank. I immediately recognized the Asian features and fired. Hit him in the head. I repeated the shot. A second Red Army soldier scurried around the rear of the T34. Before he could fire his PPSch, I took him out with a hit to the chest at heart level.

The engineer was now at the tank. He heaved the concentrated load onto the back of the T34, turned around and ran back in my direction.

The turret lid of the tank opened. A head was visible. I fired. I don't know if I hit the tanker.

They came out of the darkness at the same time as my shot. A wall of living bodies came out of nowhere and moved toward the ditch. The "Uräähhhh" from dozens of throats had a paralyzing effect. I couldn't tell how many Red Army soldiers there were, but it felt like hundreds. The wave split. A larger group was now heading straight for us, while the others infiltrated the trench warfare. Bodies clashed. Knives and bayonets flashed. Close combat. The terror of all soldiers. The fight where you see the whites of your opponent's eyes. The Red Army soldiers charging in our direction reached the height of the T-34. The concentrated charge exploded.

Boom!

The detonation was gigantic and echoed several times. The 3 kg blast burst the steel of the T 34 like cardboard. The turret was literally lifted off the ground. The tank ammunition also exploded. Splinters flew around. Sparks flew and a bright jet of flame shot upwards. The attack of the Russian soldiers was stopped. The explosion stopped the wave. Two or three Russians were killed, some seriously wounded.

I pressed the butt of my rifle into my shoulder and fired shot after shot. I tried to remain as calm as possible, remembering the words of the weapons master, who advised me to fire one shot less, but to score only hits.

"Don't rush," I kept telling myself, my knees shaking terribly. I was scared.

"Hoorayaaaa!" suddenly rang out behind me.

Apparently more and more Landser had come through the ditch. They had obviously gathered in the squadron and were now being led into the counterattack by a lieutenant I didn't know.

The acrid smell of burning oil was spreading. In the darkness you could see the black veil clouds in the glow of the burning wreckage. Dark and bizarre, they hovered like shreds over the wreckage and corpses.

I could only think of one word to describe them. Death veil!

I stared at the pioneer. To my relief, the burly man stood up. I stood up as well and hurried in his direction. He nodded. "Well done! Thank you!"

The acrid smoke hurt when I breathed in, so I croaked: "You too!"

Then we rushed after the lieutenant, whose platoon we were now in the Soviets' rear. The engineer had long since picked up his spade again. I stopped for a moment, started shooting, but quickly gave up. I couldn't tell friend from foe in this crowd.

I was more afraid than I had ever been in my life and hesitated to follow my comrades. Nervously, I took the rifle in my left hand and fumbled for the pistol.

Groaning, rattling and clanking, screaming and wailing. It all mixed with the gunshots and MP volleys to create a nightmare of background noise.

A small group of Red Army soldiers broke away from the crowd and ran back. They came right at me. I was in a state of shock. Although I held the 08 in my right fist, I was unable to act. I stared at the three Russians, transfixed. One of them held his carbine forward like a spear. The bayonet was pointed at me. The distance got smaller and smaller. Only when I heard the rattle of a submachine gun behind me, and the Russian flinched when he was hit by the bayonet, did I fire my weapon. I hit the man closest to me twice in the torso. He stumbled in the middle of the run and lay on the ground, twisted in a funny way. The third Soviet also fell victim to a volley from the sniper. I turned around. It was the sergeant who had run the other way across the trench. His face was covered with blood. He came to me.

"Are you all right? You hesitated a long time, comrade."

"Everything's fine," I stammered.

He walked on. I slowly followed. The melee was decided. Our men were able to push the enemy back. Gradually, the fire died down along the trench.

Medics scurried about, bandaging the wounded on the spot and carrying them to the assembly points.

Sergeants gathered their squads, officers their platoons. The radios and field telephones in the company command posts went into overdrive.

A combat-ready force was immediately assembled to pursue the Russians. Strong flank security was also to cover the evacuation of the wounded.

However, both proved to be extremely difficult and almost impossible. The pursuit was stopped just before the next factory building by heavy machine-gun and artillery fire.

Rescuing the wounded proved to be a suicide mission for the medics. Even at dawn, the men with white armbands emblazoned with the Red Cross were still scurrying through the rubble. The "Strippenzieher," as the telecommunicators were called in the Landser jargon, scurried through the ruins with tools and reels of cable, immediately trying to lay cables so that the connection, and thus the flow of information, between the front troops and the command posts at the company, battalion, regimental, and division levels worked as well as possible.

As that bloody, bitterly cold night drew to a close, I was summoned to the company CP by a dispatcher.

Lieutenant Hübner looked anything but fresh. Like everyone else, he was completely exhausted. Nevertheless, he was constantly gathering information and passing it on to reporters or his subordinates. The officer's uniform was covered with blood. I concluded that he had been involved in hand-to-hand combat.

I sat down in a corner of the ruins and waited. After a short time, my eyes closed and I dozed off.

When I was awakened by a light tap on my shoulder, it took me a moment to fully regain consciousness.

Huebner looked at me. "Back again?"

"Uh ... yeah. I must have dozed off. I'm sorry..."

He interrupted me. "All right. I want you to find a good spot, watch the enemy, and take out any worthwhile targets that come your way. Especially officers, snipers and machine gun nests!"

I didn't answer, I was probably still a little dazed from being half asleep.

"Did you hear me?"

I silently repeated the words of the order and nodded. "Got it!"

"When it's dark, come back here!"

"Yes, Lieutenant!"

Hübner turned around. "Maracek! Have you finally reached the reserve? And is the transport of the wounded working?"

While the sergeant answered, I got up and left the company command post.

Over the next two days I managed two kills. The first kill was at dusk on the first day. I was lying on a pile of rubble, or rather on or in the pile of a collapsed roof. Protected by the tangle of roof tiles, steel girders, and beams, I had a relatively good view of two building complexes occupied by Russians. Both were about three hundred meters apart. Between them was rubble, a railroad track, and a wagon. I concentrated on the area between the two ruins because there was always movement there.

I spotted a figure. It was scurrying from cover to cover. The Red Army man was agile and extremely cautious. Sometimes he would crouch behind a pile of rubble for minutes before moving on to the next cover. I could see through the binoculars that he was carrying a messenger bag. I set the binoculars aside and took aim with the rifle. The first time I looked through the binoculars, he was gone. I was about to put the rifle down when I spotted him again by chance. He had made it from the last pile of rubble to the wagon. From there it was only 50 meters to the ruins he wanted to reach. It was five to seven meters from the wagon, behind which he was waiting for a good opportunity to run, to the next suitable cover.

I figured he would stay in that safe place for a while and then sprint the rest of the way in the dark.

So I left. I would only have a few seconds to get this shot. Meanwhile, the twilight was working for the detector. The darker it got, the harder it was for me to see him.

I began to put myself in the shoes of the enemy. All I could think about was the final stretch from the car to the ruins.

I would wait. Or don't you have time? Do you have an urgent message? Has your officer ordered you to deliver it immediately? Perhaps an order that must be carried out now, as darkness falls?

Suddenly, everything happened at breakneck speed. I recognized the movement. The Red Army soldier jumped out from behind the wagon and ran with long, fast strides to the nearest pile of rubble. My finger was already on the trigger. The body was in my sights and I pulled the trigger.

The shot whipped, the bullet racing through the twilight. At the same time as the muzzle flash, I saw the Russian fall. I drew back the rifle and waited. The urge to look through the optics or binoculars again was too great. But the fire of three machine guns shooting aimlessly in our direction kept me down. I withdrew from this position.

The second fire took place the next morning. I recognized a machine gun position and shot one of the shooters.

Picture Gallery

Sample pictures - not all are from Stalingrad, but all photos are originals from the Second World War.

All images are from the author's private archive.

P.A-0010-Feldküche - Bahnhof— Transport / P.A-0010-Field Kitchen - Station - Transportation

PA-05 - Bahnfahrt - Essen an der Schiebetür / PA-05 - Train ride - Eating at the sliding door

PA-0-G-Marschpause-Verpflegung / PA-0-G March Break Catering

PA-0-14 nach Ari-Angriff / PA-0-14 after Ari attack

PA-Serie-0-Gräber / PA Series 0 Graves

PA-Serie-0-zerstörte Stadt / PA-series-0-destroyed city

PA-0060-Landser vor dem Einsatz / PA-0060-Landser before combat deployment

PA-0-G-Feldküche / PA-0-G-Field kitchen

PA-0048-zwei Soldaten Wintertarn mit Karabiner / PA-0048-two soldiers in winter camouflage with carbine

114

PA-0043-Ju52-Flug / PA-0043-Ju52- flight

While we were able to achieve at least partial successes in our area by capturing a few buildings or sections of terrain, the attack on the main targets was not particularly successful. The Russians put up fierce resistance. Some of the buildings and factories lost in the battle were retaken.

A Russian counteroffensive was launched to drive the German troops back to their starting positions, but heavy German gunfire quickly halted the Soviet attack.

On November 12, Paulus' forces struck again. It was initiated in the morning hours by massive artillery fire. Strong infantry units then pushed forward, splitting the Russian lines, and German units stood close to the ice-covered Volga.

The southern railway station was captured by the neighboring forces at a high cost in blood, both among their own units and the Red Army. The number of killed and wounded officers and NCOs was particularly high.

The combat strength of the deployed troops fell below 50%. The generals began to warn Paul. They seemed to sense the inevitable disaster.

On November 16, 1942, the first snow fell. The east wind and icy cold did not bode well. The city was in ruins. The construction of winter shelters had been neglected and the enemy was still on this side of the Volga.

Soldiers on both sides had long since reached their limits. Emaciated and frozen, they took up positions wherever they happened to be. Surreal front lines emerged. In some of the large factory halls, only walls or floors separated the fierce opponents.

The faces of the soldiers looked cold, gloomy and haggard. The high number of casualties and the increasingly fierce fighting wore on their nerves. Those who had leave passes in their hands or were taken out of the Stalingrad area on hospital trains with tolerable wounds were considered lucky winners.

Even the seriously wounded were the object of envious glances as they were prepared for transport. Some of us would have gladly traded our health for one of these places.

On the morning of November 19, 1942, an unimaginable catastrophe loomed. With the Russian troops at Stalingrad putting up a fierce fight and unable to be pushed back across the Volga despite the most intense fighting, General Paulus had moved strong units to the front for the final offensives.

He and his general staff had failed to realize that Stalingrad had become the bait for a gigantic trap. Under the code name "Operation Uranus" the Russian military had prepared a gigantic offensive. Stalingrad was to become a death trap for the 6th Army.

At the expense of the Red Army in Stalingrad, strong Soviet troop units had been brought in, unnoticed by the Germans, to break through the enemy lines and encircle the city in a vast pincer movement.

It was freezing cold and a thick frosty fog hung over the city and surrounding area when Russian artillery fired from all barrels in the north of Stalingrad in the morning. The attack was so intense that the detonations of the heavy calibers could be heard more than forty kilometers away. Russian rocket batteries from the so-called Stalin Organs continuously fired their rockets in the direction of the German and allied troops. The howling and screaming of the Katyushas was a grueling psychological terror for the Axis, but for the Russian civilians it was the sound of liberation.

The artillery barrage was followed by an assault of heavy armor and infantry. Despite initial fierce resistance from the Romanian units, the attack could not be repulsed, and by noon on November 19, 1942, the front had collapsed.

Field telephones rang incessantly and the overloaded radio traffic required the use of every direction finder available. The reports coming in exceeded all previous fears. The Romanian front south of Stalingrad had collapsed.

The General Staff was confused as attacks were launched simultaneously on all fronts. The Russian pincer movement was not recognized at that time. Paulus did not react, as the Soviet offensive was the responsibility of Army Group B, which in turn was awaiting instructions from OKW and thus from Hitler personally. This loss of time and the misjudgement of the overall situation by General Paulus and his staff had fatal consequences.

It was not until the evening of November 19 that the German attacks on Stalingrad City were halted. It was necessary to react to the new situation as the Romanian front had completely collapsed in the meantime. German divisions had to turn back and take care of securing the flanks.

During the night of November 19-20, 1942, Russian engineers, in true suicide missions, had cleared minefields south of Stalingrad, including in the area of the flank secured by Romanian troops. On November 20, 1942, powerful Soviet armored units pushed through these gaps and overran the Romanian forward positions in the dense fog at lightning speed. Wave after wave of ground troops followed. Driving snow set in and made the defense more difficult. The Romanian units tried to resist the overwhelming enemy, but they had no chance.

It was not until November 21 that General Paulus and his staff realized the encirclement was imminent. Troops were hastily deployed to retake lost positions and to keep open the escape corridor near Kalach.

The response came too late. Kalach itself was too weak to offer sufficient resistance to the attackers. The Russian attack wedges united at Kalach on the Don on November 23, 1942, closing the ring around the German formations there.

The 6th Army was now in an encirclement battle.

That evening, Paul personally radioed that they were surrounded. He received word that relief was on the way.

The next morning, November 24, 1942, Hitler declared that the fortress of Stalingrad must be held at all costs.

On November 27, 1942, General Paulus, through his Department I a of Army High Command 6, telegraphed a general order to his soldiers, to be given orally from the regimental level up.

"Soldiers of the 6th Army! The army is trapped. This is not your fault. You held out until the enemy was at our backs. We placed him here. He will not achieve his goal of destroying us.

I still have much to ask of you. Toil and hardship in the cold and snow. To stand firm against any superior force!

118

The Führer has promised help. We must persevere until it arrives. If the whole army stands together as one, we'll make it!

So hold on, the Führer will throw us out."

The promised Luftwaffe supply of the kettle failed from the start. Only some of the 500 tons of supplies needed daily, such as food, fuel, and ammunition, could be flown in. The airlift achieved a supply rate of between 5 and 25 percent.

As a result, food rations were gradually reduced to as little as 60 grams of bread per man by the end of the battle.

The supply situation was catastrophic. On the day of complete encirclement, November 24, 1942, rations were immediately reduced to 50% of the normal daily ration.

The morale of the troops and their confidence in the leadership had been severely damaged. We were in a cauldron and were not allowed to break out.

The comrades who were already on their way to the train stations or airfields with leave passes were especially hard hit. The faces of these men were empty and cold. The disappointment could not have been greater. Worlds collapsed. They hastily wrote letters explaining that they would not be home for Christmas. The field post became the most important link to home. It was the bridge to their families, giving them hope and strength.

The rationing of food and ammunition set off alarm bells. Winter had finally arrived with blizzards and sub-zero temperatures.

"Get closer together!" was the motto.

"Stand up for each other and face the enemy together!" was the mantra.

"It's the same for the Russians!" we tried to convince ourselves, but the Russians were supplied by the Volga, we were not. The ranks of their fallen and wounded were filled from a seemingly never-ending cornucopia, but our gaps remained.

As the enemy surrendered, the weather struck. Freezing gales pierced every crack and crept under the uniforms.

While I was relatively well equipped with winter clothing, I saw many comrades every day who were still walking around in their summer uniforms. Some older soldiers told me about the same dilemma outside

119

Moscow and reported mass frostbite. Their worst fears were far exceeded weeks later. As many men would fall to the frosty fist of the Russian winter as to Russian bullets.

Hardest hit were the Russian prisoners of war. While we Landsers had hardly anything to eat, the Russians had nothing at all. Their death rate was high. Even outbreaks of cannibalism were tolerated.

The little soldier paid a high price for the stubborn mistakes of those in charge, who sat in their heated living rooms, ate three times a day and made great speeches, while we died miserably out here in Stalingrad. If there was a place that most resembled hell, it was Stalingrad.

We had long gotten used to the sound of the artillery. When it was quiet, we were constantly bombarded with slo-gans and music. It was always the same grueling chant, repeated thousands of times:

"Every seven seconds a German soldier dies in Stalingrad! Stalingrad mass grave!"

Then there was music. A tango.

Soon they did not know which was better. Russian artillery fire or loudspeaker attacks. One claimed lives incessantly, the other was very hard on the soldiers' psyche. Those who could not ignore these bombardments had to go crazy at some point.

At first we still believed in the rescue and the promised relief.

"Manstein will knock us out! General Hoth and his tanks will blow up the ring from the outside!"

But there were also promises of supplies from the air, and these did not materialize. For this reason, I stopped believing in rescue soon after the Cauldron was formed. For better or worse, I resigned myself to my fate.

I often lay awake. Shivering with cold, I pondered whether it was right or wrong to report to Barras. I had long since suppressed my lovesickness. Compared to what moved me every day, it had degenerated into a pitiful remnant of regret.

Repression is probably one of man's survival strategies. Nourished by the hope of rescue, we dug in. We had gone from attackers to defenders. The ravenous wolf had fallen into a trap and was now the hunted.

The Russians struck a fatal blow. Stalingrad lay in the fist of its namesake, the Russian head of state and army, Joseph Stalin. He only had to squeeze it to crush us. That's how it seemed to me.

The Red Army soldiers usually attacked at dawn. They came out of the icy fog or ran towards our positions in the middle of the drifting snow. Wearing white camouflage uniforms, they were difficult to spot. Mines and tactically placed machine gun nests stopped many of the attacks. Dozens of Red Army soldiers often lay bloodied in the rubble. As the attacks subsided, the moans and groans of the wounded could be heard. Some of them tried to drag themselves back to their own lines. Others were lucky enough to be rescued by medics. Those who were not rescued died in the cold. Frozen corpses lay in the embattled streets and houses.

At night the enemy continued to come in small groups of up to ten men. They usually threw two or three hand grenades into the occupied houses and then stormed in, firing from their machine guns. Or they used flamethrowers.

If the Russians captured a house, it didn't take long for us to storm it again. If we lost a position or a bunker during the day, we took it back in the evening.

After a battle, the first thing we did was to search the pockets of the fallen for food.

When it was quiet in a section of the front, fear set in, because then there was usually a Russian sniper opposite, who was supposed to take out the German machine-gun nests, officers and NCOs. The fear of a single shot far outweighed the fear of a firefight in a skirmish. A single shot always meant certain death.

A war of nerves!

Information on enemy sniper activity was gathered and immediately reported to the companies, which in turn informed the battalion. Our own snipers were deployed accordingly.

My job was to track down these snipers and eliminate them. I was also supposed to shoot officers and NCOs. Covering attacks was another job.

We copied what the Russians called the rat war approach to house-to-house fighting. It was the only adequate means of retaking buildings with minimal casualties.

121

So we also formed squads of up to ten men. Two-thirds of them would provide cover fire, while two or three brave comrades would venture forward, throwing hand grenades into the houses and then storming in.

In the cellars or in the walls of the ruins, the sharpened spade was always at hand. For the men at the front, hand-to-hand combat had become a daily routine. The primary targets were the head, face, and neck of the opponent. Secondary targets were kneecaps and wrists.

Soldiers became blunt. Mercy was banished. War was harsher and more ruthless than ever before. Humanity was extinct. Survival depended on how brutal and merciless you were in battle.

You also had to remain unharmed. With the shortage of supplies, there was not only a lack of food, fuel, ammunition, or fuel. There was also a shortage of medicine and bandages.

Like the other troops in the cauldron, the wounded were underfed. In addition, they were increasingly succumbing to the freezing temperatures and simply freezing to death.

Only those who could be flown out of the Cauldron were saved. To do so, you had to be considered a specialist or, if you were badly wounded and could be saved, you had to be given a transport pass.

I was returning from a two-day mission. A Russian machine-gun nest had taken up position on one of the upper floors of a ruin, and its firepower prevented any attack on the building. At the same time, it covered the advance of smaller Soviet combat groups and troops storming the neighboring houses. It had become a nuisance to the second company and five men fell victim to it. Only one survived, but his legs were blown to pieces. To get to the machine gun nest, I had to advance at night with a squad. They took a previously lost building in hand-to-hand combat and I scurried up to the roof. There I took up position. Despite my winter clothing and sheepskins, I was so cold that I didn't think I could get a good shot. As the machine gun covered another Russian attack, I realized their secret. They were lying under steel beams and firing through a small slit. The fire was directed by an observer. In a firefight, I would have the confidence to fire several shots. Surely no one would notice me. I paid my respects to the machine gun crew. The next day was the day. A group of Landsers attacked and came under fire from the machine gun.

They work almost like snipers, I thought to myself as I shot first the observer and then the machine-gunner.

When the gun was fired again a short time later, I shot the sniper as well. After that, the machine gun fell silent. The company moved forward and the front line was straightened out.

As I said goodbye, I somehow realized that this situation would not last long. Capturing, losing, and retaking positions, houses, or sections of the front had become the norm in this city of the dead.

In one of the balconies, our pioneers had dug some bunker-like caves into the earthen walls. Here we were relatively well protected from the Russian artillery shells. The entrances were lined with wooden planks and the doors were made of wooden slats. There were no windows.

One of the bunkers was the company command post and the infantryman's office. The others were used for sleeping and recreation.

The bunker I was in was about 20 square meters. The furniture was very sparse. I slept on straw sacks and sat on a large table and two simple benches. On the wall in the far corner was a mirror. Beneath it was a stool with a washbowl. However, there had been no hot water for some time, so personal hygiene was kept to a minimum. Beards were growing on the faces of the soldiers. Many thought it was an added protection against the cold. Only a few soldiers still resorted to shaving. And if they did, it was perhaps once a week.

There was no stove, but the temperature was at least above zero, so it felt pleasantly warm. The air in the bunker was stuffy. A few Hindenburg lamps provided diffused light.

"Ah... our master marksman is back," Sergeant Maracek greeted me.

"Close the door," growled Corporal Pfefferlein. He had been with us for two weeks, as he was still too weak to go to the front after recovering from pneumonia. Pfefferlein helped the saboteur with his paperwork or helped Maracek.

I closed the lattice door, waited until I got used to the light, and then put my rifle down at my sleeping place.

"Did you make it?" Maracek wanted to know.

"You take out one MG nest and the next day there are three new ones," Pfefferlein said.

"Yes!" I answered the sergeant's question.

"How many kills was that?"

"I don't know," came out spontaneously.

123

I secretly knew it was numbers 15, 16, and 17. I didn't count the Russians killed or wounded in battle. I only put on this one special list the men that I, as a lurking sniper, selected as targets and shot.

"It's better this way," Maracek added.

I lay down on the straw bed, wrapped myself in my woollen blanket and closed my eyes. I was hungry and dog-tired.

"Then you won't get a medal," I heard Pfefferlein say, but I didn't react and quickly fell into a deep sleep.

When I woke up the next day, there was a lot of commotion in the bunker. The men were laughing and joking. Such an exuberant atmosphere was very unusual. I raised my head curiously. "What's going on?"

"Get up, you rascal."

I recognized the voice at once. It belonged to Wohlleben, our spit.

Everyone was laughing and in a good mood. Something had happened.

Something very good must have happened, I thought, getting up and going to the table.

"Sit down here. We're celebrating the upcoming liberation!"

Still dizzy from sleep, I scratched the back of my head.

"Liberation?" I stammered.

"Please don't remove the lice until after breakfast," Pfefferlein laughed, pointing at my head.

My bladder squeezed. I was very curious and wanted to hear the whole story. "Wait, I'll just do my morning business and then you can tell me everything in peace."

Fifteen minutes later I was sitting at the table with the others. In the bunker were Hofer, Zerberich, Maraczek, Pfefferlein, Wohlleben, and Gründel, Holler, and Schneider, who had been assigned to the group with the machine gun because their platoon no longer existed.

"They were all killed in action or in the hospital for a long time," Wohlleben had said at the time of their integration.

I was poured a lukewarm and extremely thin coffee substitute, which at that moment tasted better than any coffee bean I had ever drunk in my life. I was also given two slices of bread, very thinly spread with liver sausage. A feast! I grabbed it greedily, took a bite, and chewed with relish. Despite my great hunger, I ate slowly.

I was very curious, and the good mood of my comrades was contagious.

"Has a plane with sutler goods arrived? Or is there some other reason to celebrate?" I asked, deliberately avoiding the word liberation.

Wohlleben's deep voice drowned out the chatter of my comrades. "Manstein's knocking us out!"

I didn't quite understand what he meant at first and took a sip of my granary coffee.

"That's what the Führer promised."

"Our tanks are rolling in. Hoth pushes the Iwan away and runs straight for the cauldron. Do you understand, boy? It won't be long now, and we'll have plenty to eat and drink again!"

Everyone cheered. "To Manstein!"

"When is it? Must we rush out to meet him?"

Pefferlein spoke up. "Hoth can't be that far away. There are reports from the outposts that they can hear the roar of battle from time to time."

"Guys, I bet we're going to eat a fat goose for Christmas," Maracek beamed and held out his hand.

No one intervened.

"You would have done well. I would have won the bet!"

I cleared my throat. "Maracek, I would have gone in already, but what would I do with your ass if I won?"

Everyone roared. Even Maracek himself began to laugh out loud.

Wohlleben patted me on the shoulder. "Well done."

I tried to remember the last time we had sat together so boisterously. It had been a long time. It seemed like gallows humor. I was immediately reminded of our situation. We had been sitting in a cauldron for more than three weeks. The promised air supply didn't work. The food rations had been reduced to a minimum and were not enough to keep a man healthy. We had all lost a great deal of weight. Hunger had become a constant companion.

The hunger was exacerbated by the extremely cold winter. Both together were worse than the Russian. I couldn't prove it with figures, but I had the feeling that we had more casualties from malnutrition and its consequences in connection with the extreme weather conditions than from the enemy.

Sick notes came in every day. There was a shortage of everything. I looked around. Was this madness or was rescue really imminent?

"Did you hear me?" Wohlleben's bass voice brought me back to reality.

"Uh... no," I stammered, feeling blindsided.

"I was just saying I have another surprise for you."

I was astonished. "What?"

The spittoon held up a letter. "Field mail has arrived. Here..." he handed me the envelope, "... this is for you."

I took it with trembling hands. I read my name and the return address three times. The letter was from my parents. I felt hot and cold inside. Although I was hungry and had gotten into the habit of celebrating the little food we had been given in the last few days, I ate quickly, drank the cup empty, and had only one thing on my mind. Reading. Wordlessly, I got up and went to my straw bag. I dug out my flashlight and turned it on. Meanwhile, a thick lump had formed in my throat and I felt like crying.

I began to read by the light of the lamp. It was my mother's handwriting. I felt comfortably warm and miserably cold at the same time. When I finished, I started again from the beginning. Only gradually did I understand what it said.

My dear boy,

I hope you are well. Christmas is coming soon. Maybe you can get a vacation. That would be nice.

I have some sad news for you. Your uncle Josef had a heart attack and died a week ago. We buried him yesterday. Everyone was there. Even Aunt Hilde came from Vienna.

Everyone sends their regards. Your father told everyone how proud he was of you and made a bet with Uncle Karl that you would be awarded the Iron Cross before the end of the year.

Please take care of yourself.

Unfortunately, I have something else to tell you. After you joined the army, your friend Edeltraud Eder enlisted as a nurse at the front. She also went to Russia. I met her mother yesterday. She sadly told me that Edeltraud was badly wounded in an air raid and died of her wounds.

Please take care of yourself. God bless you, my son. Please write to let me know if you are well and if I should send you anything.

Your loving parents.

126

She wrote the letter just before the siege.

Thoughts raced through my mind. Questions arose.

Why did she report to the front? Edeltraud. My great love. Did she do it because of me or because of him?

I was confused and the pain I felt continued to spread. It was like an invisible hand grabbed my neck and squeezed.

No! It was over between us. She had chosen the other guy.

Thoughts raced back and forth.

She succumbed to her severe wounds after an air raid, I finally repeated a few times in silence.

The shock was followed by emptiness. I don't know how long I sat on my straw bed staring ahead. It must have been several minutes. Maybe even half an hour.

Pictures of happy days flashed by. I saw Edeltraud's laughter, heard her voice, and then suddenly it rumbled in my head and she was lying on the floor, covered in blood. I closed my eyes, silenced my thoughts, and felt an irrepressible rage rise up inside me. It surged upward like the lava of a seething volcano.

"The Russians killed the love of my life!"

"What?"

I was torn from my thoughts. The spit had spoken to me. Because I didn't answer, he repeated his question.

"Miller, I'm talking to you. What did you say? I didn't understand you."

"Uh..." I stammered. "That's all right. I was just thinking out loud."

"Bad news from home? Is everything okay?"

"My parents," I replied somewhat monotonously, "are worried about me. And one of my uncles died."

"Sorry!"

"That's okay. I hardly knew him," I replied quickly, trying to avoid more questions. I wanted to jump up and run away. My Edeltraud was dead. My already broken heart turned to dust and ashes.

My parents had suffered for weeks. My God! I hadn't even thought of writing to them. I was in a tank and they feared for my life every day. They had written the letter before the encirclement and mailed it. It was a miracle that it got to me at all.

I salute our air force and the pilots of the Ju 52.

127

I had to write to them. At least a few lines. To let them know I'm okay.

When letters go into the kettle, they come out.

I took up my last thought and asked the spit a question: "Does the field mail also work the other way?"

"Silly question. Of course it does! Every old Auntie Ju who lands here takes off again."

I sat down at the table again. "What do you think? How long will it take Manstein to blow up the boiler from the outside?"

"Hm..." the skewer pondered. "Hard to say."

"Before Christmas! I'm sure of it," Maraczek interjected.

"Yes, before Christmas. And I'm sure they have plenty of provisions and market goods with them," laughed the young Hofer.

He was the only Landser among us whose face was free of stubble. However, this was not due to the fact that he groomed himself thoroughly, but simply because his beard growth was generally very sparse.

There was a knock.

"Yes," Wohlleben rumbled.

The door opened and a boy stood in the doorway.

"Come in, Nikolai!"

I stared at the boy. He couldn't have been more than eight or nine years old. There was something familiar about him, but I couldn't put my finger on it at the moment. The boy closed the door, walked over to Wohlleben and saluted him. Then he said in broken German, "Chäff möchtää sähen..., Oberfeldwäbel!"

"Who is that?" I asked curiously.

"Nikolai. He came to us a few days ago. His family is dead. He's nice and does all kinds of odd jobs," Maracek explained.

"And he's a bright boy. Learning our language fast. I wouldn't have put it past these Bolsheviks," Pfefferlein added.

Somehow the guy looked familiar.

"I'll go over there," Wohlleben said, getting up. "See you at lunch. I hope the horse meat soup will be ready soon."

"He gets something to eat for his services. He doesn't need much," Zerbi said.

Now I remembered. I recognized the coat with the many different colored patches. It belonged to one of the two boys I had seen looting the bodies. However, the older of the two children was wearing it at the

128

time. I could still see the picture of how happy they both were when they found the fish can.

"Where is your brother?" I asked.

The young Russian looked at me.

"Do you know him?" Maracek wanted to know right away.

"I saw him once. But there were two of them."

"I don't understand..." Nikolai replied with a shrug.

"Leave it alone, Alfred. Don't make him melancholy by reminding him of his brother. These are hard times."

I nodded and smiled at Nikolai. It's all right, son," I said.

Wohlleben walked out and Nikolai followed.

There was indeed a lot of horse meat in the soup. As we all know, taste is a matter of opinion. In the old days, we would probably have left this soup and complained to the kitchen bull. But in these days of hunger, the soup stew was like a feast. Even though the sparse vegetables in the soup had dark spots, we ignored them. When you're really hungry, you're not disgusted by slightly rotten or moldy food. We devoured everything we could find.

The spit talked non-stop and poured out news to us. "Captain Greiner got it too. He was so sick with dysentery that he died in the hospital. Our lieutenant Huebner was promoted to first lieutenant. And just imagine, Weinberger's cheek bullet caught fire. They had to cut a pretty big chunk out of the poor guy."

"For God's sake. He's so young and then so disfigured," Zerbi clapped his hands together. "He can take pity on you."

"He could have," Wohlleben continued in a hushed voice. "Unfortunately, he was so weakened by the inflammation that he died in the military hospital despite the operation."

There was a moment of silence. We thought of our dead comrades, but death had become a constant companion for us, numbing us. Dying was as much a part of everyday life as brushing your teeth or going to the toilet.

"Stalingrad - a mass grave! Ivan is right. We're all going to die here," Holler breathed out.

"Are you crazy?" Maracek poked him in the side. "Looks good to me!"

Holler had turned up the collar of his coat and pulled his cap low over his ears. His brown eyes looked tired. "We're talking ourselves up.

We're eating an emergency-slaughtered horse in a watery broth enriched with rotten vegetables. We sit in a hole in the ground without a stove, we haven't washed in days, and the lice are eating us up. More comrades die in the hospital than on the battlefield. That out there ..." he raised his hand and pointed to the exit of the bunker, "... is no longer a city, it's hell!"

Wohlleben walked over to Holler and put a hand on his shoulder. "You should lie down for a while, comrade. There are days when everything is just too much! I know that. Maracek knows it, and everyone else has been there."

"They're making wood at home now. We cut down the trees this time of year," Holler continued, not reacting to the spearman's words.

"They'll be back next winter. I promise you that. You'll cut the trees, choose the Christmas tree, and when you come home, it will smell like cookies.

Holler got tunnel vision and did not respond to his comrade's comforting words. "I don't know how many Iwans I've killed, and yet their ranks don't seem to be thinning. There are more and more of them. I have the feeling that for every dead Ivan there are two new Russians. This must stop. I want to go home.

Zerbi whispered in my ear: "He's getting the fever of the front. We have to take care of him."

Holler stood up while the corporal was still talking. "I'm suffocating in here. I need some fresh air," he said in a monotone.

"Good idea," Wohlleben grinned.

There was a knock. Nikolai called from outside. "Feldwäbel ...!"

"I'm coming."

Holler opened the door, looked at the young Russian, drew his .08 pistol from its holster, pointed the barrel at Nikolai, and pulled the trigger. The sound of the gunshot rang in his ears. "Another Ivan down."

"Nooooo!"

"Hooooo...ller!"

The bullet pierced Nikolai's left eye and exited through the top of his skull. Blood spurted out. The boy collapsed instantly.

The machine-gunner turned to his comrades. His gaze was blank. Wohlleben rushed to him, but before the gunner could reach the confused soldier, Holler shoved the barrel of the .08 into his mouth and pulled the trigger. A bloody mass of cap, bone, and brains smashed against the wood of the open door. Holler collapsed dead.

Everyone had jumped up.

"Bloody hell!"

"What an asshole!"

More comrades ran up in a flash. The door to the command post flew open as well. Two rearguards and Lieutenant Huebner came running out, saw the group of soldiers, and ran over.

Wohlleben tried to explain the situation in as few words as possible. Huebner nodded with every other word. When he finished, there was a shocked silence.

"Make sure the two bodies are buried."

"Yes, Lieutenant."

The officer turned to the men. "Is there anyone else among you as unwell as Holler?"

No one stepped forward.

"I'll ask again. Who is not feeling well? Is there anyone else among you who has been overcome by gloom?"

No one stepped forward.

"Men! We've all reached the end of our tether. We are defending ourselves against an overwhelming enemy whose reserves do not seem to be dwindling, but believe me, salvation is at hand! We are tying down so many Russian troops that it will be child's play to break the ring from the outside. It will only take a few more days and General Hoth's tanks will put the Ivan to flight. Hold out! Only a few more days!"

"Why don't we run to Hoth and break out?"

Huebner's answer came like a shot from a pistol. "Because that city bears the name of the Russian supreme commander. And if Sta-lingrad falls, so will Russia. We've been trapped here for weeks and months, and we've lost many brave men. Their deaths will not be in vain. In the name of all the fallen, I tell you that we will hold out here until help arrives. We will wear down the enemy!"

They muttered.

Two medics came running up.

"Too late. Both dead," was shouted at them, and they slowed down.

At Wohlleben's command, they lifted Holler onto the stretcher and placed the boy on top. A brief explanation followed. Then they carried the bodies away. What remained were the bloody stains on the floor and blood splattered on the wood of the door.

Huebner stepped closer to Wohlleben, leaned into his ear and whispered: "I've got half a bottle of schnapps over there. Get it and share it

131

with the men here. And then I need Miller. We got a report of increased sniper activity."

"Understood."

I decided not to write a letter home that day. I didn't want to describe the actual circumstances, nor did I want to lie about them. Stalingrad was and remained what it was. A city of the dead, a city to die in, and a city without mercy. The devil came and went here, sowing misery and ruin, and death rode through the streets as a savior.

"I can't give you much, Miller, but at least you'll have enough food for three days, provided you use it sparingly."

"Thank you, Lieutenant. I appreciate it."

"I'd rather you made sure the Russian snipers retreated as a thank you. The first company is desperate. Three food carriers, two signalmen and a sentry in only two days. That's too much even for Sta-lingrad!"

I nodded.

"Our company will take the position tomorrow night and relieve the comrades there. I know it's Christmas Eve tomorrow, but it's no use. We have to get out of there. Since the Volga has frozen over, the Soviets can bring more supplies across the river by boat than before. If you can take out the Russian sharpshooter or sharpshooters who are rampaging along our section and then cause trouble for the enemy, I'll send you on leave as soon as the cauldron opens! Decorated with the Iron Cross. I promise you that."

"Thank you, First Lieutenant."

The order came in handy. I needed to get out of the bunker, away from my comrades. I needed the solitude. While they lay in their positions, I wanted to grieve in peace, away from them, to let my thoughts wander into the past and gradually accept reality as such. I needed time. Time alone. Time to realize that Edeltraud was dead.

Something new arose as well. An irrepressible rage against the Russians. They killed my Edeltraud and I wanted revenge. I wanted to hunt them down in my pain. I blamed them for what had happened. I didn't think about who was really to blame for the misery all over Europe. I repressed it. Only every once in a while questions like

Who invaded whose country? Why do I have to kill people I've never seen before? What am I doing here?

132

I dressed and went outside. The freezing cold didn't bother me at that moment. I pulled my woolly hat down over my ears and set off. No matter where I looked, I could not see anything euphoric anymore. The glory of the once invincible Wehrmacht had long since faded. Wherever I looked, all I saw was misery.

Cursed war! Cursed Stalingrad! What have you done to me? What have you done to us?

I was wandering around without a goal. There were ruins and destroyed buildings everywhere. Some ruins were inhabitable, others were used as garbage dumps. From time to time, Landser searched a few uninhabitable ruins, looking for something burning. Two sappers broke open a large cupboard and loaded the wood onto a sledge.

A short distance away, Russian aid workers were clearing a road. Three trucks were waiting with their engines running. One of the drivers got out and looked at one of the tires.

"Damn, rotten one. Now it's losing air!" I heard him grumble loudly.

The passenger joined them and they both examined the bike. One of them reached into his coat pocket and pulled something out. "You want a Papirossi? I pulled one out of a dead Ivan's pocket earlier."

"You can smoke that stuff yourself. It just makes me sick. You better worry about the tire. I hope we make it back here with this thing. I don't feel like unloading the bodies."

As I heard the last words, I looked down at the backs of the trucks. It was a gruesome sight. It was indelibly etched in my memory. They were loaded with dead bodies. They seemed to be all fallen German soldiers. Frozen arms and legs sticking out bizarrely. The sight of bloody red stumps and battered faces sent shivers of disgust through my body. My stomach threatened to revolt. You could have seen so much suffering and misery. You could rush forward among the corpses and body parts or watch them with binoculars if you were lying in wait, but you would never get used to it.

Three trucks of dead comrades. Three trucks full of individual fates.

How many will there be? Fifty? Fifty families will mourn. Fifty comrades will no longer suffer.

I walked on. Although I didn't want to look, I turned my head again. I noticed that some of the men were missing their boots.

133

My first thought was that others must have needed warm winter boots. We are beaten and waiting for death, the second.

At some point I lost my way. I decided to go back. The field police weren't kidding when they caught you away from the troops. You were quickly accused of desertion and sentenced to death by a hastily arranged court martial. At least in the worst case. To avoid getting lost, I took the same route back. The trucks were gone and the road was passable again. I could feel the cold and wanted to get to the bunker as soon as possible.

Two comrades were standing right in front of the balka. They were jumping up and down to warm themselves. They seemed to be talking to each other. I knew one of them. When he nodded at me, I remembered who he was.

"Hey, buddy," he called to me, waving me over.

He was originally with the Tross and was a trained barber. I had gotten a haircut from him once. That was just before we went to Stalingrad. At that time we all received cigarettes as market goods. As a non-smoker, I always exchanged mine for useful things. I gave him a pack for his haircut. The only thing I couldn't remember was his na-me, so I greeted him with: "Hi, you're the barber."

"Yes. Do you need a haircut? Can you offer me something for it?"

I shook my head. "I'm sorry."

"Do you have any cigarettes or liquor or anything like that?" the other companion asked.

"Unfortunately I don't have anything."

"We could give you a really hot tip," said the barber.

The other one supported him. "And something that should be worth something to you."

"Like what?"

They looked around briefly. "We know where you can find something for your dick. A good-looking Russian woman. She'll do you for a slice of bread or two cigarettes."

"We know where she lives. She's guaranteed clean. No STDs (*Sexually Transmitted Diseasesor*) anything."

"And very pretty. Really big tits."

"Well, do you fancy it?"

I looked at them both. "How many comrades have you sent to your lady already?"

"Come with me, let's talk about it in peace," the hairdresser suggested. "If you go to the Wehrmacht brothel here, you'll only get the clap or
sack rats. Even the officers' brothel is ..."

"Not interested. Sell your whore to someone else," I interrupted. I
didn't like the whole thing. I didn't like something in the face of the
countryman I didn't know.

"I'm sure you have something in your pocket. Come on, empty your
pockets."

I took off my gloves and opened my coat. As the barber grinned at
the other in anticipation of a kill, I reached for the gun holster and pulled
out the .08. I held the barrel to the head of the soldier I didn't know.
"You're two big assholes! We're all stuck in this shithole together and you
want to steal from your own comrades! I should put a bullet in both of
your heads or hand you over to the field gendarmes, then I'll have two
bullets left for the Russians."

"Why do you have a pistol under your coat as a common soldier?"
stammered the barber.

"Because I don't carry my sniper rifle everywhere!"

"That's a mistake. We didn't mean to take anything away from you,"
the man with the barrel of my rifle to his forehead said in a low voice.

"You two piss me off!"

"The Russian woman is real. I'll tell you where to find her. Come
on, I'll show you. I even have two cigarettes left. I'll give them to you!"
cried the barber.

"First of all, I don't feel like getting anything, and secondly, I just
found out that my fiancée is dead. Fallen for Greater Germany. She was
a nurse at the Eastern Front! And then you two assholes come along and
offer me to do it with your Russian whore! Disgusting! Or are you forcing
her? I think I'll report you!"

"No! Please don't! We won't force her! Honestly. I swear it!"

"He's right. Natasha will do it to anyone who gives her anything!"

"Get the fuck out of here! Fuck off and never let me see you near
me again!"

They both immediately turned and ran away. I put the gun back in
my pocket, buttoned my coat, put on my gloves and went straight to the
bunker. I was very angry and debated whether or not to tell the Spit about
what had happened. By the time I reached the dugout, however, events
were unfolding so rapidly that the unpleasant incident became irrelevant.

"Alfred, it's good that you're already here. We've been looking for you. The Russian sniper struck again this morning. He shot Kre-mer!"

"What?" I replied in shock. "What was he doing up there?"

"He was scouting positions and routes for Hübner."

The loss of my squad leader hit me hard. Kremer was a fine man who always led the group as if we were all his younger brothers.

"Where was that?"

"Where we're supposed to go tomorrow."

"Can you be more specific?"

"You'll have to ask Maracek."

Wordlessly I went to my place and packed everything. The ration, which was supposed to last three days, was barely enough to feed a grown man for a day. Although I was always hungry, I did not feel it at that moment. My hatred for the Russians had grown immeasurably.

"What are you doing?" asked Zerberich.

"Zerbi, leave me alone."

"When you're angry, you make mistakes," the lance corporal warned.

"Huebner gave me the job of watching out for the Russians' sniper activity anyway."

"Yes, but not until tomorrow, when we all have to take our positions."

"Who cares?"

"Tomorrow is Christmas Eve. If we're lucky, the Russians will leave us alone. We'll make ourselves comfortable. No matter what it looks like there."

"Comfortable?" I laughed contemptuously and turned away.

"Alfred, don't do anything stupid."

I didn't answer, but searched my mind for the right words. Only when I had packed my things did I turn to Zerberich. "Zerbi, don't worry. I feel more comfortable if I have a bit of a head start. Then I can clear the way for you. Do you understand? I'll go to Maracek and have him show me the places where our people were shot. Then I'll find a suitable place and lie in wait."

Pfefferlein cleared his throat. "Well, I feel more comfortable knowing that Alfred will be in position when we move forward."

Zerbi tapped me on the shoulder. "These are the hardest times we've ever had in this damn war. We just have to hold out another day or two or three, then our tanks will be there and the Russians will run

136

away. I've hidden some more booze. I'll have it tomorrow. Come join us when we're settled in."

"I will," I said, squeezing the corporal's hand.

As dusk began to fall, I marched off. Some of my comrades couldn't stomach the horse meat stew and got diarrhea. Fortunately, I had no problems.

"See you tomorrow. Take care of yourself," Zerbi said goodbye to me.

It was freezing cold and the snow crunched under my boots. The cold crept under my winter jacket after the first few meters. I realized that I needed shelter, or at least a warm place to retreat to.

Our situation was dire. While our promised supplies from the German Luftwaffe were practically non-existent or covered only one-fifth of our needs, the opposite was true for the Soviets.

News trickled down to us from the division. Some of the news was more unofficial and clandestine. But from sources that could be trusted. On the other hand, it was just as controlled, so the news could be dismissed as unfounded latrine slogans. Depending on how you felt.

It was said that the Russians on this side of the Volga were nearly starving and had little ammunition left. Suffering the same fate as us, so to speak. The Volga was almost impossible to navigate because of all the ice floes. But then, a little over a week ago, the Volga froze over. The Russians, who are used to winter, built several ice roads, and since then the supply routes have worked better than ever. Wounded soldiers came across the river, supplies and new soldiers came to our side. While we were getting weaker, the enemy was getting stronger.

I wanted to see for myself. As soon as I got rid of the snipers, my goal was to get to the Volga and cause trouble there.

Only the hope and the knowledge that General Hoth and his tanks were near Stalingrad and would blow up the ring within a day or two gave us the strength to face the overwhelming enemy and the weather.

The fighting in the city had become fierce. Our soldiers looked brave and reminded me more of a lost bunch of mercenaries than the soldiers of the glorious 6th Army.

At that moment, a tunnel war had crystallized. The Russians, familiar with the area, crawled through the sewers and tunnels of the industrial district, breaking into houses and striking. Many houses changed hands several times in a few days. A few dead and wounded were always

137

left behind. The bodies were left in the cold snow. This rat war was more nerve-wracking for the men than an open battle. The enemy could strike anywhere at any time. Nowhere was safe.

Stalingrad - mass grave!

"The snipers hit exactly three places," the sergeant explained to me.

The dugout was relatively large. Pioneers had helped to extend it. A few steel beams supported the ceiling of the ruin before it collapsed. The windows had been filled in or blocked up so that they could be used as embrasures. The openings were covered with cardboard.

A few Hindenburg lamps provided dim light. It was stuffy but warm. Anything that could be burned was burned in an old cannon stove. However, they only added fuel when the fire threatened to go out. It was a way to conserve fuel. There wasn't much left, and I decided to look for fuel on the way. Then Zerbi and the others would have a warm place to stay.

If the Russian leaves us alone, we might even have a nice Christmas Eve, I thought, while the sergeant went on.

"The first two were shot at the front near house 56. Then two fell in the trench by the VB and our dugout, and the rest were shot on the path to the rear used by the signalmen and food carriers. That's what worries us the most. Because it means that every walk to the latrine, every walk to get food, and every walk to relieve the posts could be the last. There's a cunning Russian sniper out there, and you've got to get him, comrade".

I was shown the locations on the map. The sergeant lit a kerosene lamp and turned up the wick so that the map, which was drawn quite accurately, was easy to read.

"We don't have much kerosene left. Take a quick look at the spots, then I'll have to put the lamp out again."

I looked at the spots he had marked with his finger. Then I made a picture of the Russian's routes and considered whether he was working alone or with an observer. Then I thought about whether it was one or more shooters.

"Where did the Russian shoot last?"

"Here, on the way to the back."

He has worked his way so far. Either he, or both of them, know a secret path, or he's been hiding here. But then he wasn't paying attention when I arrived.

This thought made me feel a little queasy in my stomach.

"I'm going to lie down now and go out tomorrow, before sunrise."

The sergeant nodded. Only now did I realize that he was limping.

"Injured?" I asked, pointing at his right leg.

"No! This damn cold. I must have frozen two toes off. I'll go to the military hospital tomorrow."

"Why not now? It's nothing to joke about!"

"Tomorrow!"

I noticed the determination and kept quiet.

Hum

Rrrrt rrrrt

A crumbling hand grenade followed by a burst of machine-gun fire startled me. Instinctively, I grabbed my side. My fist gripped the handle of the 08 pistol.

"It's happening in the building next door. We've been lying in wait for three days," the sergeant explained.

"Sounds like they got 'em," grinned a corporal with a full beard. He had a patchy set of teeth and a small swelling in his mouth.

I mentally formed a picture from these clues. A blow with a pistol. Close combat! He's alive, so the Russian who knocked out his teeth is dead.

More shots, mixed with loud screams, brought me back to reality. But suddenly the silence had returned.

A few minutes later the door flew open. Two soldiers were supporting a wounded comrade. Two others were dragging a wounded Russian into the shelter.

"Your instincts were right, Harry. The Ivans were crawling through the channel, trying to surprise us in our sleep.

"We need bandages. Quickly! Gustav has them."

There was a hectic pace.

"We took one of them alive. Karl grabbed him by the collar, hit him over the head, and pulled him out of the hole before I rolled in the hand grenade."

"What happened to Gustav?"

"A splinter. He hadn't ducked properly!"

The table was cleared and the kerosene lamp lit. The sergeant fetched a medical bag. He noticed my expression. "The Russians got the medic," he said briefly.

139

The wounded man's coat and blouse were removed, then his shirt and undershirt were pushed aside. His body reeked of unwashed and unkempt. Insects and lice had left their mark. His shoulder was bloody both front and back. The corporal used a wet cloth to wipe away the blood around the wound.

"Ahh..."

"Are you okay?"

"Come on! Damn, it hurts," the wounded man groaned.

"Entry and exit wound. The splinter went through. You're lucky."

"Suture kit?"

"Give it to me! Hurry!"

"There's not much left, but it might be enough."

I turned away. The Russian prisoner was sitting on the floor, a staircase in front of him. He was about 20 years old and trembling with fear. A private stood beside him.

"Do you have him under control?" I heard the sergeant's voice.

"No problem."

"Ahh...! Can't you watch out! It hurts like hell!"

"If you moan, you live!"

"Do we have any more iodine?" asked another.

"No! Gustav must either return tonight or wait until tomorrow when we are released."

"Tell him to wait. Tomorrow our sniper will be waiting. That's safer!"

Meanwhile, the sergeant went over to the Russian. "Do you speak German?"

No answer. A punch landed in the prisoner's face. Blood ran from his nose over his lips and dripped down. He slowly raised his right hand, wiped his face with the back of his hand, and held his thumb to the affected nostril.

"And now?"

A few words in Russian followed. The Russian spoke them quickly. It was immediately obvious that he was very frightened.

"What size shoes does the Bolshwik have?" asked the corporal. He had bandaged the wound and was wiping his hands with a dirty cloth.

"See for yourself!"

He walked over and pointed to the padded boots. "Take them off!"

The sign language was clear. When the boots were in front of him, the corporal took them and checked their size.

140

"They stink just like our slippers! Man, this is a cursed place. A hot bath and delousing would be worth something."

I noticed right away that the boots were too small for the Landser.

"How many of you are there and where does this damn tunnel lead to? How often do you go through it and how many tunnels are there in this shithole?"

Question after question was asked, but the Russian didn't seem to understand anything. The sergeant struck again. Twice the fist slammed into the prisoner's face. This time at eye level. One blow was so hard that you could see the area around the eye swell.

"If he doesn't understand you, he won't answer," said the private, who had now positioned himself behind the Russian.

The sergeant lifted his right foot and slapped the sole of his boot on the Red Army soldier's toes.

"Ahh ..." he cried out and recoiled, and the sergeant struck him with his knee. The young soldier's lips split. He groaned.

"Are you going to beat him to death?" I asked.

The sergeant turned to me. "Sniper, do you have a problem with the way I conduct my interrogations?"

"I'm just saying. If he's dead, he won't be able to talk. Why don't you take him somewhere where someone speaks Russian? They can interrogate him."

"Because I hate those bastards. I've lost quite a few of my comrades and I've got a stinking rage in my belly. These sewer rats don't fight like soldiers anymore! They crawl through the tunnels, come out of the holes and massacre us. They rob us of our sleep, and then that loudspeaker babble makes me even angrier. Before I leave, I'll take as many Iwans with me as I can across the Jordan! And if I have to beat the bastard who tried to slit the throats of my people to find out, I'll do it!"

"Then you won't find out!"

"Do you know what they'll do to you when they find you, Sniper? They'll skin you alive and ram the barrel of your gun up your ass until the muzzle pops out of your mouth! Do you feel sorry for them?"

Silence.

I felt that all eyes in the shelter were on me at that moment. All the soldiers stared at me.

"My wife was on her way to the Eastern Front. She wanted to help us compatriots as a nurse. The Russians killed her. I will kill the Russians. And I know what they'll do if they catch me and identify me as a sniper,"

I replied calmly. I thought that the calmer I appeared, the more powerful my words would be.

Still silence. No one said anything. Obviously the sergeant was thinking about my words. His hand clenched into a fist and opened.

I unrolled my sheepskin, lay down and pulled my woollen blanket up to my chin. "Please turn it down. I want to sleep a little more. Tomorrow I have to track down the Russian snipers. It's exhausting.

"The boots fit me," one of the men said happily. "And they're a lot warmer than I thought.

"Keep them, this one won't need them anymore," the sergeant replied in a hushed voice.

"Give him yours," said the lance corporal.

The lance corporal, wearing the wadded boots of a Red Army soldier, walked over to the prisoner and took off his boots.

"Get dressed," the sergeant ordered.

The prisoner complied.

"Heinz, take him outside."

The corporal grabbed the Russian and pushed him toward the door. The sergeant followed. A minute later a shot rang out. The two soldiers returned. "Shot on the run."

What does this Stalingrad make of us, I asked myself and tried to fall asleep.

I got up early and set out. I used the sketch the sergeant had given me to find my way through the tangle of rubble. I stopped at every corner of the building and behind every pile of rubble, pausing to observe the area. Finally I found a good spot. A lamppost had been carried away by a fallen wall. It acted like the roof beam of a house. It was a bit awkward to crawl in there, but you were very well camouflaged. A small cavity had formed under the pole, large enough for me to lie down and squat. Although I still had to tuck my head in a bit when squatting, I was able to move around and stretch out enough for my blood to circulate if I stayed there for long.

The field of view in front of me was ideal. The spot was one of two neuralgic key points where the enemy had to pass, or rather appear in my field of fire. Unless he was moving through the sewers, but I didn't think so.

The snow also had an insulating effect. It wasn't nearly as warm as in an igloo, but at least I felt a pleasant difference in temperature.

Good thing the east wind wasn't blowing in!

I unrolled the coat and started to unpack my backpack. Three empty tin cans were for the toilet. I laid out the ammunition.

Two more of the explosive rounds.

Then I put the 08 next to me. I wanted to have it on hand in case of an emergency. Next I put the scope on the rifle. The barrel was wrapped in a dirty white sheet. I slid it through the sight slot and glanced over the possible field of fire. Then I adjusted the sights to the intended range. I put the rifle down, picked up the binoculars, and began to observe.

My shelter was not far from the dugout where Zerbi and the others would relieve the sergeant. To our left were some completely destroyed factory buildings, to the right was a larger area. Obviously no man's land.

Rails, destroyed wagons, a burned out locomotive. A few ruins.

A sniper could hide anywhere.

I pulled out the sergeant's sketch and placed it in front of me. Then I looked at the terrain in front of me, turned the sketch around so I had the Russians' point of view, and tried to imagine the area I couldn't see.

I put the pencil on the places where the sniper had shot our comrades and drew a radius. I compared this with the actual events and the hiding places there.

I planned and thought non-stop. After an hour I came to the conclusion that the Russian could be anywhere. My idea was useless. I certainly couldn't find out where he was hiding. Especially since, like us German snipers, he would probably change position after every shot or stay in his hole and make himself invisible for a while.

They work in pairs, was my next thought, but that didn't get me very far either. It could be an observer and two or three snipers. The Russians were masters of sniping.

This thought made me uneasy. If there really were several snipers, they would most likely spot me with the first shot or, in the worst case, even before my first shot.

My position was good. Very good, in fact. I could see no man's land, the Russian side and a small part of our positions. I didn't think about the fact that I could be very close to the Russian-occupied houses on the right flank when I moved into the small cave. I crawled to the back and looked for something to block the entrance. I spotted what looked like roofing felt and pulled on it. Since it was frozen, I braced myself against it and literally tore at it. Eventually a few stones rolled down, and I fell backwards, holding the cardboard in my hand. It had originally covered

143

a corpse. The dead man's face had been eaten away to the bone on one side. Mice, rats, feral cats, or dogs, if those animals had not already ended up in cooking pots, had feasted on him. I was overcome with disgust. I covered the entrance from behind and felt safer.

The winter had ensured that the piles of corpses had not yet decomposed.

When the thaw comes, this city will become the largest graveyard on Earth, I thought. You'll be able to smell the stench from afar, and swarms of mosquitoes and vermin will rule Stalingrad. Hopefully we'll be able to send the Russians across the Volga in the winter!

When I was back in position and took a closer look at the terrain, I recognized the large number of fallen soldiers lying around. It was a scene of horror.

Until the afternoon nothing happened. Absolutely nothing. My stomach slowly recovered from the disgusting shock of the gnawed corpse and growled. I unwrapped some dry biscuits and began to eat. I bit off small pieces at a time, chewing very slowly.

The more I ate, the hungrier I got. A glance at my ration told me that I had two thin slices of bread a day. I also had a tin of sardines in oil and a small tin of ham sausage.

"Three days," I muttered, hoping that General Hoth would bring plenty of food to Stalingrad with the tanks.

With the hours I spent in the position, I realized that I couldn't stay here permanently. I had to go back to the dugout to warm up. I would set a time slot, look at my watch, and after the last biscuit was eaten, I would go back to the position.

The process was always the same. I mentally divided the terrain into small grids and looked at each section to identify any changes that might indicate sniper hideouts.

Many things went through my mind while I waited. The meaningless and the meaningful alternated. I remembered playing soccer with my classmates and how the ball ended up in our teacher's garden. He didn't give it back to us, but locked it in his shed. On Sunday mornings he always went to the pub and played cards. We arranged to meet him, climbed over the fence and got into the shed by breaking out two rickety wooden slats from the side wall. Once we had the ball back, we put the slats back in place. Then we peed in the teacher's carp pond, climbed back over the fence, and ran as fast as we could to the soccer field. We laughed and celebrated our victory. But we were all sick to our stomachs when we had to go back to school on Monday. Well, he hadn't noticed, and we were the bravest boys in the whole fourth grade. A smile crossed my face at the thought of that time. My heart warmed for a moment.

I also thought about how I ended up on the Eastern Front and why I was destroying lives with a sniper rifle. A year ago, I would have bet house and home that I, Alfred Miller, could never do such a thing.

Feelings are funny things. One moment they make you feel high and fly to heaven, and the next moment they drag you down to hell. In my case, it was great heartbreak that sent me to the front. In retrospect, my mother was right. It was complete nonsense to volunteer for the military for something like that. It was too late now. I was here. Here in Stalingrad.

Who knows where I would have been otherwise. The draft would have come sooner or later anyway. Hm ... maybe I would have been in France or Africa. No matter. I'm here now and I have a job to do. There's a Russian sniper sneaking around somewhere, shooting my comrades one by one.

At some point I also reached the point where I became fully aware of our situation. I didn't need to delude myself. Despite all the euphoria with which we were fooling ourselves, I had to admit that we were at the end of our tether. I felt that I had been treated somewhat unfairly in terms of food rations. Nevertheless, I had lost a lot of weight and hunger had become a daily companion. If I looked in the mirror, what would I see? A skinny guy or a strong soldier?

Think of something else, I told myself.

Time passed very slowly that day and I found myself looking at my watch at shorter and shorter intervals.

The stretch before me was quiet. Even after several hours there was still no movement. This was atypical for a front line in this hellish city. I felt that something was brewing. There were two possible explanations for the silence. Either the Russians were preparing to attack, or a sniper was waiting for his shot. The unspeakable silence was an unmistakable sign.

Quiet, much too quiet, I kept thinking, and I stayed in my position longer than I had originally planned. There isn't a square meter in Stalingrad that isn't constantly being fought over. Something is wrong here. They're out there somewhere, squatting and waiting. I'll get you!

The cold had long since crept through all the cracks in my little position and was inexorably eating its way through my winter uniform.

145

By dawn, I was exhausted from the concentrated lurking. Hunger and cold took their toll. Nevertheless, I pulled myself together and tried to concentrate for a few minutes for the last time that day.

At dusk, the deer leave the shelter of the forest to graze in the meadows and floodplains. This is the moment when the hunter strikes.

With this in mind, I pulled out the binoculars and began to visually scan my grid. However, I selected the terrain and focused my attention on a few places that I thought would be particularly good for snipers.

Where are you?

I had braved the sub-zero temperatures for a long time, but now the time had come. I was cold and shivering. I realized that I probably wouldn't be able to get a good shot off.

After searching more than half of the neuralgic points, I heard something. It sounded like the rumble of a stone rolling down a pile of rubble. Then there was silence. It was absolutely silent. Eerily quiet. There was nothing to be heard. I set the binoculars aside and listened intently.

Many things could have caused this.

Still the deceptive silence.

The horizon was already gray and about to merge seamlessly into the darkness of the night.

All right, one last look and then I'll call it a day.

I picked up the binoculars, looked for the spot where I had stopped my search earlier, and was startled. I recognized a movement. Something had moved aside. The hairs on the back of my neck immediately stood up and a shiver ran from my neck to my toes. My heart began to race. The residual light was just enough to make out enough. I had him. He was on the second floor of a ruin. The front wall of the former hall was almost gone. Snow had been blown into the ruins. Before, everything in this area had been covered in white. Now something dark was visible. Upon closer inspection, I suspected that it was a large pipe. Or maybe it was a cavity, similar to the one I was lying in. But with the huge difference that my opening was permanently open to the front, while the one opposite me must have been closed.

A board, a cardboard box or an umbrella. He can use anything. A small hole is enough for observation, and he has to put this screen aside for the shot.

Be that as it may, only now, with the onset of darkness, had the sniper dared to push aside the hatch, the cover, or whatever it was.

146

It's just one of your positions. You've shot from here before, my friend, but this time it will be your last shot. Show yourself!

Suddenly, I felt neither cold nor hungry. I had waited all day and had finally reached my goal. The hunting fever had seized me.

Were you lying there for hours? No, you must have a well-hidden entrance and crawl into position from behind.

I picked up my rifle, pushed it into position, rested the butt against my shoulder and looked through the sight. A tiny correction followed, then I was on target. I had to pull myself together to take the shot. I realized there was only one shot. After that, I had to pull back. It was the only way I could continue to use my hiding place. Besides, I couldn't survive the cold night without catching a cold or getting frostbite. Either could mean the end of my sniping activities. Maybe even my death.

Concentrate!

Although I knew where it was, the target was very difficult to make out in the twilight. I had probably the most difficult shot of my sniping career so far.

I took off my right glove. I was still wearing wool gloves under the thick mittens. I had cut off the index finger of the glove on my shooting hand. I had a difficult shot ahead of me, so I thought about loading an explosive bullet. I estimated the distance to my target to be a good 400 meters. Maybe twenty meters more or less. I was freeze-framed and an accurate shot was difficult. While I was still thinking, my hand automatically went to my coat pocket. I clumsily pulled out one of my last explosive rounds. I had to hurry. Soon it was dark and the target was barely visible. Despite my clammy fingers, the bullet was loaded and in the barrel in no time. I pressed the butt against my shoulder. My right eye stared through the sight, my index finger on the trigger guard's pressure point.

Suddenly I heard voices. Soft whispers. They were unmistakable snatches of words in Russian. Regardless of the temperature outside, I felt a shiver run down my spine. A few more stones rolled down the pile of rubble. Another whisper followed, then the sound of boots. Panting and metallic clatter.

They are attacking. They're right beside me. The sniper's covering them!

I was scared. Scared to death. What was I going to do? If I took out the sniper, it would only be a matter of time before they found me and massacred me. If I didn't shoot, I'd have their backs, but my comrades' lives would be in danger.

147

Maybe it's one of the squads smoking out the houses, then they have a flamethrower and set fire to the pile of rubble I'm lying in. I don't want to burn!

I was shaking like a leaf, not because of the cold, but because of the fear of death. My hand searched for the gun holster.

"The last bullet is for you," the words of the weapon master echoed in my head.

To shoot or not to shoot?

Panicked thoughts raced through my mind. Did I cover the entrance to my hiding place well? Would the Red Army soldiers get past it? Could the Russian sniper see me if I crawled out the back and returned to my own positions? Could I get past the Russians at all?

Damn it. They took out the outpost!

I was sure there was another outpost between me and the Russian positions. The sergeant had mentioned it.

They cut the throats of the two men, I guessed.

Anger mixed with my fear of death. What was I going to do? More thoughts followed. Could they fire a single shot?

If they ambushed my comrades and took the position, Zerbi and the others might walk into a trap. Or they could simply be targeted by the Russian sniper.

Either way. I would be in enemy territory. I would have to hold out here until my comrades retook the positions. That could take days, or it might not happen at all. One thing was certain. If the Soviets found me here in a day or two, they would torture me to death.

I was paralyzed with fear. Nevertheless, I had to make a decision. I looked through the optics. The remaining light was just enough for a good shot. It could be over in a few minutes. Then the hole where the Russian was hiding would be barely visible. Unless he fired and the muzzle flash showed me the way.

Pure adrenaline coursed through my veins. I had less than a minute to make one of the most difficult decisions of my life. My heart was racing, my pulse was pounding. Beads of sweat formed on my forehead. I could feel my armpits getting wet. All this despite the freezing cold.

I couldn't turn around in my position. If I had to leave, I would have to crawl out backwards. The Russians could grab me by the boots, drag me out, and massacre me slowly.

Die like a hero or die like a coward!

I cursed this stupid hero talk.

There are no heroes, only men who act with cautious calculation based on their abilities, or who are tired of life and are done with it all.

I pressed the butt of the Mosin Nagant to my shoulder and took aim at the area where I had spotted the Russian sniper.

It's almost too dark. Damn it! I must have thought too long! I wonder if a shot is appropriate? I'm an idiot! No matter! I have to try. No! I don't have to try, I have to do it. I have to do it. I have to finish him!

The pipe, or rather the opening where the sniper was hiding, was barely visible. There was a deceptive silence at that moment. Every street, every house in Stalingrad was being fought over or fought against. Planes from both sides flew wave after wave of attacks. The guns and tanks were barely silent, and yet I couldn't hear the noise of the battle in this section of the front, I was so focused on my target. Instinctively, I had probably subconsciously blocked out everything around me.

The explosive round was in the chamber. I was ready to take out this sniper who had killed so many of my comrades. Highly concentrated, I took aim at his hiding place. I thought I felt movement, but I stayed stubbornly on target. My index finger curled. I felt the pressure point.

Show yourself! Show yourself at last!

Time was working for him. I breathed shallowly, ready to pull the trigger.

Show yourself!

I was not mistaken. I saw him. He was dimly visible. Like a shadow flitting along a dark wall, yet recognizable by its movement. He had probably identified a target and moved into position. The last resistance of the trigger guard had been overcome. I pulled the trigger. The shot broke the silence and echoed back. The butt struck my shoulder. The muzzle flash gave away my position. Against my sniper's instincts, I did not retreat. I stayed where I was and continued to stare hypnotically through the scope.

Let them shoot me. At least it'll be quick.

Not a shot was fired. No one shot at me. I realized that my target was lying there calmly. I had got him. A direct hit!

I chased the hunter down and killed him.

At that moment I felt like a victor. For a brief moment, I was a winner.

A rumble. Voices! Hectic hissing orders.

A machine gun rattled. A flare shot up and a bright magnesium light flickered in the sky. I pulled the gun back and crawled back a bit myself.

My heart raced with excitement. The front was waking up. Gunfire and the noise of battle increased. My first instinct was to pack up and fight my way to the dugout. I would have fallen to the rear of the group of Red Army soldiers, and I might have killed a few of them, but I would have been exposed not only to their gunfire, but also to the fire of my own men.

If they had discovered my hiding place, I thought to myself, they would have smoked me out long ago.

I decided to lie down and wait. My heartbeat began to normalize. The cold came back. It had never really gone away, but I hadn't noticed. Now it was creeping through all the seams, eating through my uniform and covering my skin. I shivered and kept moving my fingers and toes.

After about half an hour, the fighting died down. The Russians who had passed my hiding place didn't come back.

Either they liked it or they found another way.

I paused in shock as a third possibility flashed through my mind.

Or they have overpowered my comrades and are sitting in the heated shelter instead.

Without a second thought, I packed up. When I was done, I listened attentively outside for a few minutes. Everything seemed to be fine. I waited for a moment to consider if I should stay, but the freezing cold left me no choice. My longing for the warmth of the heated shelter outweighed my dread of running into the arms of roaming Red Army soldiers.

Holding the 08 pistol in a tight fist, I crawled out backwards, shivering more with fear than cold. I expected to be grabbed by my legs and dragged out by force or shot. I also expected a blow to the spine and wondered if I should point the .08 at my head and pull the trigger.

Nothing of the sort happened. I was outside, looked around and got up. I immediately put on my backpack and rifle and started walking. I had memorized the route very well in case I had to retreat quickly. I crawled to the nearest ruin. I was afraid that the Red Army soldiers might be hiding behind one of these walls of rubble.

They must have gone somewhere.

I was driven forward by a mixture of mortal fear, euphoria at my success, and the need for a warm place to stay. I moved with extreme caution, watching my steps. The cursed, icy wind increased. It whipped against the exposed skin and felt like a sharp knife slicing through the surface.

I scurried from cover to cover and from ruin to ruin. When I thought I heard something, I ducked behind a section of wall. As soon as I ducked, I was scared to death. A Red Army soldier was lying beside me. A machine gun had almost severed his right leg below the thigh. A pulp of blood, red flesh and bone oozed out of his shredded uniform. The ground was red.

The dying man twitched his stump a few more times. But his face remained unchanged. It showed a pained expression. Instinctively, I pointed the barrel of the .08 at the Russian, but I quickly realized that this twitch was nothing more than the last reflex of his nerves.

He bears a certain resemblance to Weinberger, I realized.

After the initial shock had passed, I immediately searched the Red Army soldier's pockets.

Empty! Bloody hell! His comrades are just as hungry as we are, I thought.

I waited a little longer and watched my enemy die.

Why are we enemies? We see each other for the first time in our lives. Somewhere in Russia a mother will soon be crying and a brother will go to war full of hatred for the Germans.

The questions and answers were repeated. I closed my eyes, took a deep breath and walked on. The weather was getting to me. The cold almost paralyzed me. It ate through my clothes and began to become unbearable. I was glad when I finally approached the shelter. A warning call rang out: "Stop!"

I was startled. I hadn't expected that. Stop! I was lucky. There were enough comrades who didn't scream, but shot at once.

"Don't shoot! It's me. Miller! The sniper!"

"Parole?"

"You idiot! I don't have a slogan! But what kind of Ivan speaks in Styrian dialect?" I raged.

"Then come here slowly!"

I stood up and walked to the post.

"When you go in, tell the sergeant that we have to cut the relief times in half. I'm freezing to death."

"I'll fix it."

The stench that hit me was enormous, but it didn't bother me. It was warm. I immediately went to the stove, took off my gloves, and rubbed my hands in the warm air that was escaping. I had to keep telling

151

people about the fire. I was asked several times if, because of the darkness, I was sure that I had actually taken out the Russian sniper I was looking for. I patiently answered each question, reassuring my comrades with precise details backed up by the evidence I mentioned. I drank a cup of warm water and felt tired. I heard the sergeant discussing post times with his men. Then I slipped into the land of dreams.

When you think of Christmas, you think of roast goose, decorated Christmas trees, lit candles, and brightly wrapped presents. You see smiles on people's faces and the smell of cookies.

Christmas 1942 in Stalingrad was far from romantic. Under the command of Lieutenant Huebner, our entire unit had been moved forward. Even the cavalry and the military hospitals had been checked again in order to get a more or less reasonable number on paper. The entire company consisted of 40, maybe even 50 combat-ready men. But these soldiers were already at the end of their tether. They looked emaciated, undernourished, and tired. The soldiers' expressions were blank. Only a few had not stopped laughing and joking. Maybe they did it because they couldn't help it and it was their way of thinking, or maybe it was just to escape reality and not go crazy in the face of our situation.

Hofer and Zerbi had greeted me warmly when they arrived. Pfefferlein nodded politely at me as well. The three new men with the machine gun were silent. Then there were two new men in the group whom I knew only by sight. One was a square-jawed fellow who reminded me of the burly pioneer. They could have been brothers. The other was the opposite. He looked a little slender and very young. He had probably joined the troop with Hofer. In any case, they were always talking.

The three machine-gunners, Gründel, Holler and Schneider, were so happy that the bunker had a cannon stove that they set out in the morning to collect wood.

They returned around noon. The men were shivering with cold and exertion. They had loaded a lot of fuel on a door that had been converted into a sledge. A small layer of ice had formed on their coats. Ice crystals clung to their hats and beards. The thermometer had dropped to minus 30 degrees.

I had to smile when I saw the loaded sled-like vehicle and was delighted. We didn't have much to eat, but at least we wouldn't freeze. Finding the fuel was a great success. Stalingrad had been destroyed, and fuel

152

was as valuable as food in this Arctic winter. Warmth meant life. Accordingly, we greeted the three soldiers with great joy.

In no time the booty was loaded into the shelter.

"The painted parts will really stink," remarked Gründel, one of the three machine-gunners.

"Better stabbed than frozen to death," commented Zerbi, and out of defiance he immediately stoked the fire with one of the paint-covered wooden parts.

"Won't the smoke give us away?" Hofer wanted to know.

His eyes showed fear. When my companions arrived, I noticed that Hofer had changed. Not only was he a few pounds lighter, but the joyful expression, the youthful, carefree glow had disappeared. Hofer seemed empty, tense, and at the end of his physical and mental tether. I was worried about him.

"Pi pa po ... there's smoke coming out of every corner. The Russians are shooting blindly at everything anyway. We could just as easily burn oil and send black clouds into the sky, they wouldn't choose us as their primary target," Zerbi reassured us.

Half an hour later we were sitting together. The wood crackled in the stove. Although it was relatively warm in the ruins, the biting cold seeped in through a series of gaps and cracks. We took off our coats only to warm them briefly by the fire and to remove the lice from time to time.

Pfefferlein had made something like an artificial Christmas tree. He had nailed five slats of different lengths to a wooden pole. The longest was at the bottom and the shortest at the top. Small candle stumps were attached to the left and right with wax.

"Later Lieutenant Hüber and some others will come by. The spit let it be known that there's something special for today," said the lance corporal after he had set up his structure and proudly inspected it. "So I thought I'd create a Christmas atmosphere."

I went to the stove and poured some hot water into my mug. On the one hand, we were all looking forward to Christmas. It was probably the hope of a brief escape from reality. We imagined this holiday as we knew and loved it. But try as we might, there was no particularly pious Christmas spirit here in the shelter.

A few men hunkered down to work on the lice, while the others stared ahead, tired and exhausted. Outside the cannons rumbled dully.

"Will Ivan attack today? The Russians know we celebrate Christmas. They might take advantage of that."

Zerbi made a contemptuous gesture. "The Ivan will be sweating because General Hoth is closing in with his tanks. The Bolsheviks will be working on their escape plans."

Pfefferlein laughed. "That's a wish I'd like to put under the tree as a present and unwrap later."

I warmed my hands on the mug and sat back down on my bed. Hofer got up and came over to me.

"Can I sit with you for a while?"

"Sure," I replied.

"When do you have to go stalking again?"

I thought about it. "Hm ... I can't say for sure. I caught the Russian bastard. Now they think I'm lying in wait. They'll probably move very carefully."

"That's good."

Hofer spoke in a low voice. I immediately realized that no one was supposed to be listening to us, so I began to whisper as well. "Something is bothering you. Speak up. Today is Christmas Eve, so it's okay to let go of all your burdens."

"I saw something the other day."

"Like what?"

"We were on a tour. We searched the ruins. That's where we found the Russian hideout. Just women and children."

"And?"

"Pfefferlein picked out one of the women and pushed her into a corner. He put the gun to her head and grabbed her skirt."

"That bastard!"

"Then he started to unzip his pants. The children were crying and the other women were moaning. I told him to stop, but he just laughed and said that the Russian women would love it.

I immediately thought of the German nurses and the Russian women who had made friends with the Wehrmacht soldiers. This was frowned upon by our leadership, but it happened very often.

What will happen to them if the Russians defeat us?

"Did he rape them?"

"No. Zerbi called us. We had to get out immediately and go back to the shelter. Pfefferlein cursed and swore. Then, out of sheer rage, he punched the Russian woman in the face with his fist. I told Zerbi all this

154

right away, but he just waved it off and said it was human nature and you can't sweat your guts out ..." he swallowed, "... I think that's the order of the day. This Stalingrad has turned us into wild animals," he continued.

I was shocked. I had expected a different reaction from Zerberich. What had happened to us. Without saying a word, I got up and went over to Pfefferlein. I grinned at him and pointed to the tree. "Nicely done. Does it remind you of home?"

He nodded with a wide grin. "I always get the biggest fir from the forest for my wife and children."

"Well, when you rape defenseless Russian women, do you think of your wife and children? And when the Russians defeat us and take your wife, do you want your children to watch?"

Pfefferlein's face turned white. He jumped to his feet, clenched his fists and shouted: "You miserable dog! I'm going to report you. This is the subversion of military power! The Russians won't win. And if you take my wife..." He stood in front of me and grabbed me by the collar.

"Stop!"

Zerberich's powerful voice rang out. At the same time, Holler and Schneider jumped up and grabbed Pfefferlein. There was a commotion in the dugout.

"Have you two gone mad? What's going on?"

Pfefferlein looked for Hofer. His look was filled with hatred.

"If you harm a single hair on his head, I already know my next target."

"Shut up, both of you!" scolded Zerbi. "Shake hands. Today is Christmas Eve! And remember one thing. We need every single man. If we start tearing each other apart, the Russian will have won. We won't have to hold out much longer. The cauldron will soon be blown open. So pull yourselves together and don't make life difficult for a few Russian women."

I froze in shock. Zerbi looked at me. He recognized my disappointment.

"Nothing happened."

"And if it had, what would you have done? Take him to court for rape or say we need every man?"

"You would have seen it already. And now let's forget the whole thing."

I went back to my seat. Only now did I realize that I had ignored Hofer. "I'm sorry about that. I was just upset!"

155

The young soldier breathed deeply.

"That's all right. At least it's been brought up now and the men know about it."

He stood up.

"If you try that again in my presence, I'll shoot you!"

Pfefferlein grinned and started to answer, but Zerberich immediately spoke up. "If I hear anything more about it, he'll be on guard all night. And if the boss comes later, I don't want to hear another word about it. Otherwise I'll be unpleasant. Do you understand?"

No one said anything.

"I want to hear it. Do you understand me, or does someone want to go to the post office right away?"

"Yes," grumbled Pfefferlein.

"And you?"

"I understand," I said.

Hofer nodded as well. "Everything that needed to be said has been said."

The mood remained depressed. Even when Wohlleben came into the dugout and handed out half a bar of chocolate and an extra slice of bread as a Christmas surprise to each man, there was no real joy.

"If you think that's all, you're wrong," said the spitfire happily. "Maracek and the boss are bringing ten more cigarettes for everyone. All the old man had to do was go back to the company's command post. A dispatcher ordered him there in a hurry. There's probably some news.

The candles on the homemade tree were burning, and four or five comrades were humming and singing a few Christmas carols. Idyllic was something else. While the people at home thought we were sitting here together in the romance of the campfire, celebrating Christmas and laughing as we unwrapped presents, the truth was that unshaven, hungry faces were staring at each other, hoping to be rescued soon from this miserable hell of Stalingrad.

Wohlleben, Zerbi, Maracek and one of the machine-gunners were playing cards. I was amazed at their composure. But I guess each of us had his own way of dealing with this extreme situation.

I sat in a corner with Hofer, and we decided to keep an eye on Pfefferlein. We didn't trust him. After we had gotten rid of our anger, something unexpected happened. Pfefferlein, who had been sitting alone

156

next to his dummy tree for half an hour, came over to us. His look was no longer angry. In fact, he seemed a little distracted.

"I don't know what happened to me, but what I did is not who I am anymore. This city, this killing, this hopelessness, all of it has turned me into an animal. I must apologize to you. Today is Christmas Eve. I think this is the right time to reflect."

As soon as he said it, he turned and went back to his tree. We looked at each other. Hofer leaned into my ear and whispered. "Do you think you can trust him? Is he really serious?"

I thought about it, I didn't know what I believed. "I can only hope so."

We sat in silence. I took my chocolate and started to eat. I broke off piece after piece with relish, letting each one melt on my tongue. When it was almost gone, I pushed a small piece of bread after it. I closed my eyes and thought of home.

When Lieutenant Huebner came to us in the dugout, his expression was anything but cheerful. As icy as the wind that blew in from the outside with his arrival was the news he brought with him bluntly and all too clearly. The officer took off his gloves and walked over to the stove. He rubbed his hands in the warm air that came out. Huebner's submachine gun hung from the belt across his back. The ice that had clung to the weapon was thawing and dripping.

He'll need oil to keep it from rusting, I thought, staring at our company commander.

"Comrades, soldiers..." he began in a rough sounding, slightly cracked voice. It was clear that he had something unpleasant to tell us. The attention was accordingly high. All eyes were on Lieutenant Hübner. "...we face an uncertain fate!"

Wohlleben put the cards aside. "Cursed and sewn! I don't suspect anything good," he muttered.

Huebner cleared his throat and came straight to the point. "General Hoth had to turn back with his tanks. The Cauldron will not be opened from the outside. There will be no relief, and we will not break out ourselves, but hold the Cauldron to the bitter end. That is the Führer's order."

Stunned silence.

"They're not going to let us die here, are they? First Lieutenant, that was just a bad joke on your part, wasn't it?" grumbled Gründel.

Hübner's look left no room for doubt. He definitely meant what he said. Goose bumps formed on my neck and spread all over my body. The spark of hope that had carried us Landser to this day and made us accept all the hardships, this spark of hope burst, dissolved and burned into nothing. All that remained was death and misery.

"No, gentlemen, I'm afraid this is no joke. It's the bitter truth."

"Well, do me the honor, it's getting dark!" Wohlleben commented. "A fantastic Christmas present from the Führer. This ..." The first sergeant was interrupted by the company commander.

"Wohlleben, there is no point in complaining. And our laws still apply. You are an example to the men. Don't forget that."

"With your permission, Lieutenant. I have a brother-in-law from Braunau. He's the biggest bovine under God's heaven. I was just thinking about that fool and the other idiots from that godforsaken backwater."

Hübner reached into a bag he had brought with him. "Here you go. Merry Christmas," he said in an unmistakably sarcastic tone, slamming ten packs of Juno cigarettes onto the table. "This is all we have left."

Wohlleben, who had been joking and laughing confidently since the beginning of the cauldron, seemed completely overwhelmed from one moment to the next. He reached into the bag in which he had carried the chocolate and pulled out a notepad. Then he tore off a sheet for each of us. Then he dug around in the bag again. Soon there were three pencils in his hand. He put them next to the paper. "I don't know about you, comrades, but I'm going to write a letter home. The Luftwaffe will take care of us. It hasn't gone so well so far, but if we're to stay here and there's no relief from the outside, they'll get us through the winter, and in the spring Manstein will roll up with his tanks. The same air force that supplies us and flies our wounded out of the cauldron is taking field posts with it. So write to your families and let them know you're alive!"

I wondered where this man got his optimism. The way he had reacted just a minute before, I doubted he was serious, but his words had an effect on the men. They grabbed onto the new spark of hope. They had nothing else to hold on to.

Huebner looked around. "Seats on the planes are limited. I remind you that self-mutilation is a death sentence. We stand our ground! We are soldiers of the Wehrmacht and members of the 6th Army. They will not let us down. And we will endure. So, men, if you have even a single thought of self-mutilation, then forget it very quickly.

158

Zerbi cleared his throat. "Well, I think it's time for me to give you my gift."

The lance corporal got up, went to his sleeping place and searched purposefully for something he had hidden well. Finally, he found a bottle of schnapps in his hand.

"Vodka! I bought it from a peasant before we left for Stalingrad. I wanted to drink it myself, but I never got the chance. Get your cups!"

That night I realized that we were going to die in this town. I didn't even begin to believe that we would last until spring. The Russians had sealed the kettle so tightly that it couldn't be blown open from the outside, much less from the inside. The air supply was not working. The food rations had been drastically reduced since the kettle was made, and the shortages due to the freezing winter and the lack of food were growing. When you looked at us closely, we didn't look like soldiers, we were a ragged, smelly bunch of exhausted, worn out, and beaten men.

And yet they would not surrender to the enemy. The fear of the hated enemy was too great.

Or is it the fear of the enemy's revenge for the atrocities we have committed? We are in the land of the Russians. We are the invaders. We have brought terror and fire to this land. The Russians will hold us responsible.

Edeltraud came back into my mind. I saw her laughing and dancing happily. Then, half asleep, an image came to my mind that made me feel hatred again. Although it hadn't happened that way, I saw a Russian raping Edeltraud, getting down on her, and then shooting her in the head. I opened my eyes, trembling with fear and rage. I had mixed reality with Hofer's story about Pfefferlein and the Russian woman. We were no better than the Russians. What was I to do?

Someone had gotten up and put a piece of wood in the stove. For a moment a red-orange light shone in the hut. Then the door was shut again. Crackling, the flames ate their way in and continued to pour out the vital warm air. One of the men snored loudly, another groaned, and a third seemed to be talking in his sleep. Or maybe he was just talking to himself. I pulled the blanket over my nose, turned to my side and tried to fall asleep.

The next morning we were rudely awakened.

159

"Get out! Everybody out!" a dispatcher yelled. He was from the company command post. Wohlleben had sent him to us. "The Ivan is on its way with strong shock troops. We've already lost two houses. We must counterattack! Everyone to the company command post immediately!"

With the door open, the room was suddenly filled with icy cold. Muffled gunshots and explosions could be heard.

"Close the door! Damn it!" Zerbi cursed and jumped up.

The detector disappeared as quickly as it had appeared.

"You heard it. Get out of here! You have exactly five minutes. If you haven't done your morning toilet by then, you'll have to do it on the way!" the corporal yelled, grabbing his steel helmet. He put it on over his woolly hat and fastened the leather strap under his chin. Then he grabbed the submachine gun and checked the magazine. As he reached for the belt and fastened it around his coat, I stood up.

Cursing and cursing, the other soldiers also struggled up from their camps. Here one hastily took a sip of water, there another shoved a last, saved bite into his mouth.

Gunshots and the sound of exploding grenades could be heard.

"Faster, you lazy bastards! Or do you want to invite Ivan for coffee?"

"He won't make it," Gründel shouted, pointing at Schneider.

Pfefferlein knelt down beside Schneider and touched his forehead. "Fever. The man is shaking all over. He must go to the hospital immediately!"

"Bloody hell!" cursed Zerbi. "Now of all times," he added. The lance corporal went to his seat and picked up a small tube of pills. "I have three more ASA. Here, take one of these. It'll bring the fever down. You stay here, and when we get back, we'll take you to the military hospital."

Schneider seemed to understand. Trembling, he tried to lift his upper body. Gründel broke the tablet in half and pushed it into Schneider's mouth. "That way you can swallow it better."

Meanwhile, Pfefferlein had poured some water into Schneider's cup. "Here."

Holler put the last pieces of wood in the stove. "We really need more fuel."

"Get out now!"

The Russians had decided to attack the outermost edge of our battalion's section and had captured two buildings. One of them was in

160

a strategic position. From there the enemy could have seen one of our main supply routes and fired at it. We also feared that he would take building after building and encircle us. We had to drive him out.

"He doesn't even rest on Christmas Day."

No one answered. The temperature seemed to have dropped again. The east wind was unbearably cold. We lay among the ruins and waited for the Soviets to attack. My job was to push the enemy to the right with my rifle and bring them in front of the barrel of our machine gun. It was also my job to locate and eliminate any Russian snipers or machine gunners. I had found a spot under a burned out tank wreck. The hulk had driven onto a pile of rubble, rolled over, and probably been hit by a grenade.

We had melted into a miserable pile. I could feel the hunger and the exertion making me weaker. Or was that just my imagination? How much longer could we hold out under these conditions?

A week? Two weeks? If we didn't die in a hail of Russian bullets, we would starve, freeze, or die of disease! If we have nothing to eat, what will the Russian prisoners get?

I had to close my eyes.

Think of something else. Concentrate on your task! There will be a solution.

The attack was initiated with light grenade launcher fire.

Wham Wham

I had already searched the area several times with binoculars, but I couldn't see anything out of the ordinary.

We were lucky. Except for one or two grenades, everyone died in the no-man's-land under the rubble. The only danger was flying shrapnel.

Then they came. I was astonished. I hadn't expected so many Red Army soldiers, because all the time there had been talk of shock troops. I estimated that there were more than forty or fifty men.

Damn, this isn't a raiding party, they're up to something!

"Urähhh!" echoed through the cold streets. Suddenly, two or three heavy Russian machine guns rattled away. One of them had taken up position on one of the upper floors of a tall building. I took aim at it.

"Let them come closer! They're not expecting us!" was the call.

There was hardly any fire yet. "Urähhh!"

I aimed at Shooter I. His face was clearly visible. I held my bre-ath, pressed the butt against my shoulder and pulled the trigger. Before I realized the echo of my shot and felt the recoil of the weapon, the Russian

161

machine-gunner fell with a blow to the head. I repeated and immediately fired at the man, who anxiously rushed to the position of the man I had hit. He grabbed his neck. Through the optics of the rifle, I could see blood spurting from his neck at intervals.

A hit!

Knowing that this machine gun would not be fired again for the time being, I swung the barrel around. At the same moment, the order to fire sounded: "Fire!"

The Russian attackers ran into a wall of steel. Ten or twelve of them fell to the ground, hit. The others took cover.

I looked for the nearest Russian machine gun and spotted it at the edge of the building. My shooting angle wasn't as ideal as before, but I took my shot anyway. I scored a hit in the right side of the gunner's body.

"Attaaaack!"

The time had come. The counterattack was ordered. The Landser stood up. The cries of "Uräh" of the Russians had fallen silent. Instead, the German soldiers shouted "Juhu!

I recognized Zerbi. He whipped the men out of their positions and charged forward with them. There was a flash from the muzzle of his submachine gun. Now the Red Army soldiers stood up. Some ran toward my comrades, rifles outstretched, bayonets fixed. Others stayed where they were and fired. A few turned and ran away.

I emptied my clip and reloaded. When I looked through the scope again, I saw Zerbi facing two Russians. He shot one of them in the stomach, and the other rammed his bayonet into Zerbi's side. I immediately shot the Russian in the head. Panic washed over me. Zerbi dropped to his knees. He dropped the submachine gun and grabbed his wound.

I shot two more Russians who were near him. "Where's the damn medic?" I shouted, afraid for my comrade.

The Russian machine gun opened fire again. I took aim and fired at a helmet. The gun was silent. I don't know if I hit it or if I just scared the shooter. A Russian officer appeared briefly. He barked orders and waved a pistol in his hand. I aimed for his stomach and pulled the trigger. He lay on the ground, screaming, his face contorted with pain.

I looked for Zerbi again, but couldn't find him.

Instead, I saw our machine-gunners. They were running across the rubble. They ran crouched and close together. Holler was a little taller and broader than Gründel. He carried the bag of supplies and a box of ammunition, Gründel the machine gun. They both took cover almost at the same time. Someone was shooting at them. I searched feverishly for the shooter and found something that made my blood run cold. I saw a Russian man with binoculars. He was watching the battlefield, moving his hand and indicating something to someone.

Snipers!

The moment he saw me and realized that I was aiming at him, I pulled the trigger. The bullet went through his binoculars and pierced his skull.

Change position, I reminded myself, and withdrew the weapon without having achieved anything. Lying under the wreckage, I reloaded. Shaking with excitement, I took a few deep breaths. Then I crawled out of the hiding place and backed down the small pile of rubble to take cover in the nearby ruins. There I would take up a new position. Running as fast as I could, I caught a stone and stumbled. Still falling, I thought: Not again! Suddenly I felt a heavy blow on my side. It immediately became burning hot. It was as if someone had stuck a red-hot knitting needle into my lung between my ribs. The pain was so intense that I did not feel the impact on the ground. I lay there gasping for breath. Everything suddenly sounded so muffled and distant. Everything started to blur before my eyes. Stars danced around. This pain. Every breath triggered it. I felt like I was exhaling a piece of my life's spirit with every rise and fall of my chest.

Whether I was the target and victim of a Russian sniper or just a stray bullet, I would probably never know.

So this is how I'm going to die. Lonely. Lost in the ruins of Stalingrad. I expected death to be my salvation.

I no longer felt the cold. Pain covered everything. At some point I opened my mouth and began to scream. I tasted blood. The sense of time and space disappeared.

At some point, shadows fell over me. Far from any perception of reality, I heard voices. Hands grabbed me. I was turned around. That sharp pain again. I screamed, or at least tried to.

"He's alive! It's the sniper."

"Go! Get in the back!"

As they grabbed me and put me on a stretcher, I thought I was going to die of pain. It all came together in my head. Pain, cold, fear. A dark wall fell on me and buried me. I blacked out.

When I came to, I was lying in the middle of a pile of wounded soldiers. Moaning and groaning. Screaming and whimpering. I opened my eyes. Diffuse light. The ceiling of the room was a dirty white. A disgusting stench surrounded me. It was a mixture of blood, intestines, urine and excrement. Everything was covered in clouds of carbolic acid. I gagged, but my stomach was empty. Even if I had wanted to, there was nothing in my body to vomit.

I had been given a pressure bandage. The blanket over me was covered in blood and full of lice. The animals immediately looked for a new body. If they were without a living host for a certain amount of time, they would die.

The wounded were brought in at regular intervals. They were either taken to the operating room or laid on their sides somewhere to die. Sometimes a doctor made the decision, sometimes a nurse or a medic.

I didn't want to die. When it was my turn, I wanted to look strong enough for them to operate on me.

Someone came in. I realized it was a doctor. He was wearing a rubberized, blood-stained apron. The doctor walked with a nurse along the line of wounded. Every now and then he or she would say: "The one on the left. Please finish him for me. He still has time..."

They stopped in front of me. I wanted to speak, but I couldn't. The doctor looked at me. "First diagnosis, a shot in the lung? Take him to the others."

"This is the sniper. He was told he was vital to the war effort. His battalion commander specifically asked for him," the nurse explained.

"If the bullet destroys too much tissue and he loses too much blood, he will die. We have..." he paused and looked at me. "Hm... that's the one where the bullet ricocheted off the rib. Maybe he was lucky. Well, get him ready. If he hasn't lost too much blood yet and the bullet didn't really go deep, we might be able to make it."

The nurse waved two medics over. "Get ready for surgery."

They went on their way. Less than a minute later, two paramedics came to me. As they took me into the operating room, I felt deathly ill. Between two tables were buckets and tubs filled with human body parts. Everything was covered in blood. I wanted to jump off the gurney and run away. I wanted to get out of here, to go home, or at least to a place where it was humane. But I couldn't move, let alone jump off the stretcher and run away. So I closed my eyes and tried to escape in my mind. I imagined home. Styria in the spring.

164

"Take off the bandage and put it aside. We'll need it."

Another voice asked, "Dazed?"

Someone fidgeted with me. It hurt.

"Do we have an x-ray?"

A woman's voice could be heard now. "He's going to make it. His pulse is strong and he has no fever."

A scream drowned everything out. "No!"

"Hold him! And where the hell is the saw?"

I knew immediately what was happening on the operating table next to me. They were sawing off part of a comrade's body. Someone was taking it and throwing it into one of the tubs.

Oh, my God! Stalingrad, you hell on earth!

At that moment I knew that my life would be over only if I gave up.

Run away! Run away, Alfred, I urged myself.

Pictures of home flashed through my mind again. I wanted to see it again, this supposedly perfect world. I turned away.

I didn't know how long I had slept. The rumble and thunder of Russian artillery woke me. I felt as if I had been beaten to death. A stone weighing several tons seemed to be lying on my chest. At the same time, thousands of lice seemed to be trying to eat me. I felt like I had run into a tank. But I was breathing. I was alive. I tried to remember.

Surgery! They took the bullet out and I'm alive!

Little by little I came back to reality.

Huiiittt Wumm

It was that time again. The Russians covered us with their artillery. The Red Army howitzers pounded the already dead city again and again. The shells once again plowed up ruins, stones and funnel fields.

Phew!

A tremor could be felt. The ground and the walls shook. Dust and lime dripped from the ceiling. The impact of a heavy shell was not far from the building where we were lying.

"That was just the tail end of a heavy suitcase. We're not in the center of the fire. The Iwans are only hitting us with their guns on the periphery."

The voice sounded familiar. I tried to raise my torso, but I couldn't. Someone pressed a letter into my hand.

"Put this letter in your pocket, Miller. I have had the battalion declare you a person of importance to the war effort. I have noted and reported your accomplishments. Whether it will work in this madness, I don't know. I can only hope so. You will be flown out of here on one of the next planes. Please take this letter and send it to my wife at home. I think if I take it to the field post office it will probably never reach my family."

It was Lieutenant Huebner speaking to me. I turned my head. The officer was sitting on the floor beside me. His uniform was covered with crusted blood. He had a bandage on his head. His eyes were closed.

"What ... what is ..."

"Quiet. Miller. You are weak. I let them take me to them. In the last battle, a Russian drew his bayonet over my eyes. I lost the left one. The doctors hope to save my right eye."

"Zerbi?" came out of my mouth, hoarse and weak.

"Corporal Zerberich lost too much blood. He didn't make it."

Silence.

"Your warm shelter no longer exists either. Direct hit! It was as if the Russians had shot at the smoke from the oven. The whole building is now a pile of rubble."

I was too weak to talk. Lieutenant Huebner talked for a long time. It did me good. Eventually I fell asleep again. When I woke up in the middle of the night, he was gone. The officer's letter was in my pants.

The food situation became more and more dramatic. The German soldiers were undernourished. Cold, disease, and hunger caused more casualties than the constant house-to-house fighting and skirmishes. The noose of death was tightening.

Nevertheless, General Paulus refused to surrender on January 8, 1943.

A week after the operation to remove the bullet from my lung, I had regained enough strength to receive the coveted note with the red stripe.

"This one is fit for transport," a doctor had said shortly before.

Even though I was lying here in the completely overcrowded hole, stinking of excrement, blood and pus mixed with carbolic acid, not knowing whether the door would open one morning and Red Army soldiers would storm in and bash our heads in, I felt hope. For the first time in a long time, the thought of rescue brought me out of the emotional hole I had fallen into. A note was pinned to me that meant life. I was fit for transport and deemed worthy of being flown out.

As the medics put me on a stretcher and carried me out, I saw a scene of horror outside the military hospital bunker. The frozen corpses of several comrades lay left and right. I thought I recognized Zerbi, but I wasn't sure. Ice and snow covered most of the face of the corpse I thought was Lance Corporal Zerberich.

How proud we had been to enter this metropolis on the Volga. And how pitiful we looked now. I had seen the real face of war. I could look into the face of the devil, and soon he would spit me out. Spit me out because I got a seat on one of the planes leaving the cauldron.

The truck was completely full. The local police accompanied us. I shook my head inwardly. We were dying, but military discipline and order were maintained to the end.

On the way to Gumrak airfield I heard many shouts.

"Comrades, take me with you!"

"You dirty bastards, don't leave me behind!"

"I want to go home!"

At one point, one of the field gendarmes even fired a shot from his machine gun into the air.

It felt like the longest and cruelest ride I had ever been on. Every rock the driver rolled over, every pothole he hit, and every curve he took hurt like hell. I was afraid of the Russian air force and the freezing cold was getting to me more and more. I wondered how long it would take for a hand, foot, toe or finger to freeze off.

There was a commotion at the airport. I couldn't see how many Landser there were besieging the entrance to the tarmac. Field generals were securing everything. There were shouts, screams, and gunfire.

The truck came to a stop. The tailgate was opened and the tarp was folded to the side. A careful check was made. Finally it was my turn.

"Where to?"

"This has to get out of the boiler! The order comes from above!"

"No more room!"

This sentence made my blood run cold.

"Who said that?"

"Me! And now back."

167

I heard the engines of the planes, saw the shadows of their wings. I was nearing my destination. Lifting my head briefly, I recognized a group of screaming and yelling compatriots. There must have been hundreds of them. They all wanted to get out of here.

Who made the selection? Who got it? Why me of all people?

"Name?"

"Are you crazy?"

"Name, comrade! I've been ordered to put this man on a plane, and that's what I'm going to do. He's a sniper and probably a war hero. I wouldn't want to be in your shoes when I report that you didn't let him through.

"Then go through and see if you can squeeze him in somewhere, you big mouth. There's no room!"

They carried me on. I heard more and more screaming.

"Faster!"

"Everybody to the side!"

They carried me right up to the fuselage of a Ju 52.

"Full up! You'll have to take the next one!" they said.

Again a field gendarme snapped at us. "Get out of here or I'll shoot!"

"He has to get out! Important for the war! Coming from above!"

"Next machine. Hurry up!"

They hurried on with me. Again I saw a wing. "Get out of the way! Damn it, make way!"

I don't know what the paramedic was told about me, but he wanted me to disappear into the belly of one of those planes.

"Stop! There's another important transport. This one has to go!"

"Come on, get him in!"

The stretcher was pushed into the plane.

"Have a good trip," the paramedic called to me.

"Full up! Close the door!"

A Me 109 roared past. It was about to take off.

That must be one of our escorts, I thought.

A short time later, our old Aunt Ju taxied into position. The pilot stepped on the gas and we picked up speed. When he pulled back the stick and the nose of the plane lifted, I thought I was saved. But soon after takeoff, I heard smaller and larger detonations.

Flak! The Russians are shooting at us. Will it ever stop?

The climb continued. The fear of being hit made me tremble. I closed my eyes, feeling weak and defenseless. It was only when we reached our standard altitude that I felt relatively safe for the first time. Then the shelling stopped. We had made it. We had escaped the cauldron. I was one of the lucky few who didn't die in Stalingrad. I had escaped the cauldron and with it certain death.

On January 10, 1943, the last major Russian offensive against the encircled 6th Army began. Codenamed Operation Kolzo, the ring of siege was tightened.

The vital airports of Pitomnik and Gumrak were captured and Stalingrad was divided into a northern and southern cauldron.

On January 30, 1943, Paulus was promoted to field marshal. The commander-in-chief of the 6th Army refused to commit suicide as Hitler had requested. Instead, after the surrender, Paulus was taken prisoner to Russia.

From January 31, 1943, the surrender of the individual sections of the kettle began. On February 2, 1943, the last German soldiers surrendered at Stalingrad. Of the estimated 100,000 soldiers who fell into Russian captivity, only about 6,000 men returned home years later.

Military historians disagree on the number of casualties during the Battle of Stalingrad. However, it is believed that about 700,000 people died. Two thirds of them were Russians.

Considering the cruel fate of the city and the victims of the battle, there can be only one conclusion.

Never again war! Resist the beginnings!

The end

Glossary for the novel:

Arko	Artillery commander
Degtyarov DP 1928	Soviet machine gun caliber 7.62 x 54 mm, conspicuous by plate magazine (filling: 47 cartridges)
iron ration	The survival rations as emergency rations for German soldiers in the First and Second World Wars were officially called eiserne Portion (iron ration). If the regular rations failed, the specially packaged emergency rations were only to be opened and consumed on the express orders of the commanding officer. However, this reservation of orders could not be upheld during the course of the war. Two iron portions per soldier were carried on the field kitchen or in a convoy vehicle. For the Wehrmacht, this iron portion consisted as standard of 300 g of bread (*a packet of hard cookies, crispbread or rusks*), a 200 g tin of meat (liver sausage, ham sausage, etc.), 150 g of ready-made food (e.g. *canned vegetable stew or pea sausage*) and a 20 g sachet of coffee powder.
Concentrated load *(original)*	Prefabricated explosive in cuboid form, dimensions: 7.6 x 16.4 x

	19.5 cm, weight with carrying ring: 3 kg explosive
concentrated charge *(several hand grenade warheads are tied around a stick grenade)*	Emergency aid for blowing up obstacles, shelters or for defending against armored vehicles *(the latter usually for blowing off chains or when attacking immobile vehicles)*
He 111 *(Heinkel)*	Standard bomber *(alongside the Ju 88)* of the German Luftwaffe in the Second World War, bomb load: 2000 kg, armament: 3 MG, crew: 5 men
HKL	Abbreviation for main battle line
Yak	Yakovlev Yak-1 was a single-engine Soviet fighter aircraft
Reich Labor Service (abbreviation RAD)	According to the Reich Labor Service Act, all young Germans of both sexes were obliged to serve their nation in the Reich Labor Service. As a rule, young men were called up for labor service for a period of 6 months before their military service. Women also made their contribution. The assignments of the RAD varied. (e.g. in agriculture or road construction)
Me Bf 109 *(Messerschmitt)*	Single-seat German fighter aircraft. Standard fighter of the Luftwaffe. Number built: approx. 33,300 units
MP 40 *also called "Schmeisser", as the name of the weapon's designer was affixed to the magazines.*	Submachine gun 40, successor to the MP 38, standard submachine gun of the German Wehrmacht and Waffen-SS, bar magazine, 32 rounds, 9 mm Parabellum

Muckefuck	noun for coffee substitute *(grain coffee, chicory coffee or malt coffee)* or for thin, stretched coffee
Pervitin	Stimulant - Manufacturer: *Temmler (1938 - 1988)*, Pervitin suppresses tiredness, hunger, pain and anxiety. Side effects: psychoses, personality disorders, risk of addiction. Initially often distributed to soldiers in the Wehrmacht as a miracle cure, distribution was greatly reduced after the side effects became known. Nicknames: *Armored chocolate, Stuka tablets*
Political commissar, political officer in the Red Army	Each *Red Army* unit *(down to battalion level)* was assigned a political commissar who had the authority to rescind orders from commanders who violated the principles of the CPSU. Although this was counterproductive from a military point of view, it ensured the political reliability of the army vis-à-vis the party.
PPSch 41 *(Pistolet-Pulemjot Schpagina)*	Russian submachine gun, (year of introduction in the Red Army 12/1940), very reliable, caliber 7.62 x 25 TT, Drum magazine (71 cartridges) and curved magazine (35 cartridges), developed by *Georgii Semyonovich Shpagin*

PM 1910 *(Pulemjot Maxima obrasza 1910)*	Russian machine gun based on the development of the manufacturer *Hakim Maxim.* Use with protective shield on wheeled carriage. Weight: approx. 24 kg - with carriage: 66 kg Caliber: 7.62 x 54 mm Cadence: 500 - 600 shots min.
OKW	High Command of the Wehrmacht
Mosin Nagant	Russian bolt-action rifle, caliber 7.62 x 54 R, magazine filling 5 cartridges with loading strip. The rifle was also available in a version for snipers, the standard rifle of the Red Army.
K 98	Mauser Model 98, German bolt action rifle, caliber 7.92 x 57 mm, 8 x 57 IS, magazine filling 5 cartridges with loading strip. The rifle was also available in a version for snipers, standard weapon of the Wehrmacht and Waffen-SS.
Scho-ka-kola	round chocolate containing caffeine, packed in a tin can.
Sanka	Abbreviation for ambulance
Sturmovik	Ilyushin Il-2 "Sturmovik", single or two-seater, single-engine, heavily armored combat aircraft of the Soviet Air Force
TVPl	Military medical area
UvD	Abbr. for: Sergeant on duty *(usually a special service to supervise the internal service, the UvD followed the instructions of the company sergeant (Spieß) and ensured compliance with military order after the end of the service.*

	Among other things, he was responsible for waking up the soldiers, supervising the performance of cleaning duties and ensuring that the night's rest was observed)
WuG	Weapons and equipment Sergeant, *usually a member of the combat team*
z.b.V.	military abbreviation for: for special use

From the general Landser jargon:

Eight-eight	German anti-aircraft gun (FlaK), caliber 88 mm, which could also be used for ground targets
Age	Nickname for: Superior officer (usually company, battalion or division commander)
Acja	Tub sledge (Nordic means of winter transportation)
Barras	Barras is the soldier's term for '*the military*'. To be conscripted means to be drafted (compulsory military service). The word probably goes back to the French statesman *Vicomte de Barras (1755-1829)*. He was one of those responsible when France introduced compulsory military service. The term is particularly common in southern Germany and Austria. A number of soldiers from Napoleon's *Grande Armée* during his Russian campaign came from these regions.
Germanic booty	Slang term for ethnic Germans *(people of German origin with non-German citizenship)*
Thunderbolt	Latrine / field toilet

Frozen Meat Order	East Medal
Goulash cannon	Field kitchen
"Sore throat"	someone would like to receive an a-ward *(Knight's Cross, Iron Cross, etc.)*
Hindenburg light (named after Paul von Hindenburg)	A small bowl filled with fat or tallow into which a wick was inserted. It was used as emergency lighting. Its modern successor is the tea light.
Assumption mission	particularly risky and dangerous assignment, the execution of which is highly likely to lead to death *(albeit unintentionally)*
Hitler saw	MG 42 = powerful German machine gun
Dog tag	Identification tag *(usually worn on a chain around the neck)*
Taxiway	Important road/supply route, e.g. for supplying troops, but also for rapid advance
Intelligence strips	Tucks on the pants of members of the general staff
Ivan	Nickname for Red Army *soldiers (Russian soldiers)*
KdF (Strength through Joy)	Nationalist political organization with the task of organizing leisure activities *(hiking, vacations = land and sea travel)* for the German population. The society was based in Berlin.
Chain dog	Nickname for: Field gendarme, recognizable by his metal sign hanging around his neck (Military Police)
puzzle cup	nailed soldier's boots
Suitcase	Nickname for: heavy grenade
Bucket or bucket truck	Light, all-terrain military car (Volkswagen)
Kitchen bull	Nickname for: Cook
Landser	German soldier *(Landsknecht = mercenary fighting on foot 15th/16th century)*

Tinsel	Medals/other also rank insignia
Latrine slogan	Rumor
Napola	National political college = boarding school leading to university entrance qualification / elite school for the training of young National Socialist leaders
Skewer	Nickname for: company sergeant *(usually a master sergeant in the position of a sergeant major - recognizable by two sewn-on piston rings on the uniform sleeve)*
Fried egg	Nickname for: *German Cross in Gold.* The *German Cross* was a German military decoration and was established by Adolf Hitler on September 28, 41 in the gold and silver divisions. It has the shape of an eight-pointed star made of gray-tinted silver. On it is a laurel wreath made of gold or silver, which encloses a swastika. Silver: *(awarded for: repeatedly proven exceptional acts of bravery or multiple outstanding merits in troop leadership)* Gold: *(awarded for: multiple exceptional merits in military warfare)*
Stalin organ	Soviet rocket launcher *(proper name in the Red Army: "Katyusha")*
String-puller	radio operator
S-Mine	Abbreviation for shrapnel mine, fragmentation mine or spring mine. When triggered by a kick or tripwire, the mine body is thrown up to about hip to shoulder height and explodes

	with a fragmentation effect. This weapon was so effective that it has found many imitators to this day.
Aunt Ju	Nickname for the Junkers Ju 52, an aircraft type manufactured by Junkers Flugzeugwerk AG, Dessau. The most successful model was the three-engine Junkers Ju 52/3m from 1932, which evolved from the single-engine Ju 52/1m model.
Twelve-ender	Professional soldier *(period of service was at least 12 years)*

Ranks of the Wehrmacht (mountain troops):

Crews and non-commissioned officers (Sergeant)

Soldier *(Jäger, pioneer, grenadier, cannoneer, etc.)*	without sleeve patches
Senior Soldier *(senior engineer, senior grenadier, senior gunner, etc.)*	a gray square star (different design depending on the type of troop)
Private	a gray angle
Corporal	two gray interlocking angles
Corporal more than six years of service	two gray angles, above it a star
Sergeant *(in the mountain troops=Oberjäger)*	U-shaped route
Staff Sergeant = Unterfeldwebel *(in the cavalry and artillery = Unterwachtmeister)*	Braid around the epaulette
Sergeant First Class *(in the cavalry and artillery = sergeant)*	like Unterfeldwebel, but additionally a four-pointed matt silver aluminum star

Master Sergeant = Oberfeldwebel *(in the cavalry and artillery = Ober- wachtmeister)*	like Unterfeldwebel, but with two matt silver aluminum stars
First Sergeant *(in the cavalry and ar- tillery = Stabswachtmeister) this rank was introduced in 1939*	like Unterfeldwebel, but with three matt silver aluminum stars
Sergeant Major (Spieß) *= not an actual rank but an official po- sition*	Recognizable by piston rings on the sleeves of the field blouse

Officers

Lieutenant *(medical service = assistant doctor)*	Collar mirror: a silver oak leaf half wreath, an aluminum-colo- red double wing and silver piping
First Lieutenant *(medical service = assistant doctor)*	Collar mirror like Lieutenant, but two wings
Captain *(medical service = staff doctor)*	Collar mirror like Lieutenant, but three wings
Major *(medical service = senior medical officer)*	Collar mirror: silver piping, a sil- ver oak leaf wreath, a silver dou- ble wing
Lieutenant Colonel *(medical service = senior medical officer)*	Collar mirror: like Major, but two wings
Colonel *(medical service = senior physician)*	Collar mirror: like Major, but three wings
Major General *(medical service = general practitioner)*	Collar mirror with a double swing arm
Lieutenant General *(Medical Service = Surgeon General)*	Collar mirror with two double wings
General *(Medical Service = Surgeon General)*	two silver stars
Colonel General	three silver stars
Field Marshal General	like Generaloberst, but additio- nally two crossed marshal's

	batons in the clutches of the imperial eagle.

Remark:

In the medical service, an Aesculapian staff was also applied to the epaulettes.

Candidate officer

OA = officer candidate

Flag officer (Sergeant) OA	like Sergeant, with a double Sergeanttresse across the lower end of the epaulette
Ensign OA	like Unterfeldwebel, plus a double Sergeanttresse across the lower end of the epaulette
Flag Officer (Sergeant) OA	like a sergeant, with a double Sergeanttresse across the lower end of the epaulette
Midshipman OA	like Oberfeldwebel, plus double Sergeanttresse across the lower end of the epaulette
Junior doctor (medical service in the army and air force)	Like the midshipman, but aluminum-colored braid edging with cornflower blue border, stars and Aesculapian staff were made of white metal

Note:

The Oberleutnant and the Unteroffizier already wore officer's uniforms with brown officer's uniform, officer's peaked cap and officer's collar tab.

179

The sniper system of the Wehrmacht and Waffen-SS in bullet points:

Sniping was very much neglected by the Wehrmacht until the attack on the Soviet Union. Only when the Wehrmacht was confronted with the Russian snipers, derogatorily called tree snipers, during the Russian War, did the Wehrmacht revert to the old Reichswehr rifles.

Initially, volunteers were trained only at the unit level (regiment, battalion, company). At the same time, the first training courses were established. Training schools were set up at various military training areas (e.g. Seetaleralpe, Zossen) and training plans for shooting instructors and sniper training were drawn up.

The Waffen-SS trained its volunteers at divisional combat schools, SS field replacement units, and SS sniper training and replacement units. Courses were also held at the SS Junker Schools (e.g., Bad Tölz), SS Unterführer Schools (e.g., Ljubljana), and SS Panzergrenadier Schools (e.g., Kienschlag).

Sniper training was generally voluntary, but good marksmen (e.g. hunters) could be recommended and sent by the company.

Much was expected of the candidates. In addition to excellent marksmanship, impeccable character, and good eyesight, snipers were expected to be quick on their feet, able to concentrate, and possess excellent camouflage and tactical skills.

Particularly in the early days, snipers were increasingly deployed at company or battalion level, with the Waffen-SS training too few soldiers and usually limiting itself to one sniper per company. The men were usually integrated into their groups, but were equipped with rifles with telescopic sights and could be called up for special tasks as needed. At the front, commanders quickly realized the enormous impact of using sharpshooters.

A few riflemen could stop an enemy attack, cover retreats, accompany their own shock troops (flank protection), or force enemy shock troops to retreat.

The sniper courses that were established lasted from three weeks to two months, depending on the type and location.

As a rule, they were taught (analogous to Wehrmacht / Waffen-SS training):

- Use of the telescopic sight (in the following abbreviated to ZF), especially aiming and aiming errors
- Construction and function of the ZF
- Identification of defects
- Adjustment of the scope
- Weapon and scope care
- Shooting theory, in particular Types of aiming, target recognition, distance estimation, effects of weather, lighting and temperature on the aiming point.
- Tactical instruction, including Combat attacks, use of terrain, camouflage and deception, working with an observer, forest, terrain, and house-to-house combat, position building, stalking, and sneak-attack exercises.
- Close-quarters and tank combat
- Training films (own training films as well as films provided by the enemy) completed the training.

Remark:

(Training plans/ documents can be found in the Bundesarchiv in Freiburg:
- RS 3-12/ 39 - 12th SS Panzer Division "Hitlerjugend
- RS3-9/ 7 - 9th SS Panzer Division "Hohenstaufen")

During the training courses, Waffen-SS sniper candidates also received weekly training in the area of "Weltanschauung". Topics included Nazism, internationalism, Bolshevism, Judaism, and the SS as a Germanic clan order. In this way, the criminal ideology of the Nazi regime was taught over and over again so that it would become ingrained in the minds of young Germans.

Those who successfully completed the course received a certificate identifying them as sharpshooters. The weapons issued during the course remained with the (successful) snipers and became part of their personal equipment.

Sniper equipment (in addition to standard equipment)

- Rifle with ZF (ZF = Rifle scope)
- Ammunition (see following article)
- Container for the ZF
- Tools and care utensils for the ZF (partly regulated in service regulations, e.g. for the ZF 39, D134 dated January 22, 1940)
- Cleaning device for the gun
- Binoculars with auxiliary apertures
- Combat knife
- A compass
- Covering table
- Camouflage helmet cover
- Camouflage sniper jacket
- Camouflage tent awning
- Camo net with mosquito net
- Camouflage Mask
- Camouflage string and nails
- Fork (padded branch fork) for rifle rest
- Winter camouflage for weather conditions

Rifle

The most common rifle used by German snipers was the Karabiner 98 K. It was also preferred to the later Rifle 43 because of its longer range and better accuracy. Various models were issued as telescopic sights, which differed in mounting, magnification or light intensity. Depending on availability, the rifle scopes (e.g. ZF 39, ZF 41, ZF 4) were selected by the shooters according to their needs and preferences.

Ammunition used - 7.9 mm (8x57lS):

S.	Pointed floor
l. S.	light pointed bullet
s. S.	heavy pointed bullet
S. m. E.	Pointed bullet with iron core
S. w. K.	Pointed bullet with steel core
S. w. K. (H)	Pointed bullet with hardened steel core (see note)
S. w. K. L`spur	Pointed bullet with steel core and tracer (see note)
S. m. L`track	Pointed bullet with tracer (see note)
P. w. K.	Phosphor with steel core
Pr cartridge	Phosphorus / incendiary projectile (see note)
B. cartridge	Observation cartridge (see note)
Various practice projectiles	

Remark:

The hit (impact) could be observed with the observation cartridge, as both a small flame and a small cloud of smoke could be seen on impact. Behind a phosphorus charge was a capsule containing lead azide or nitropenta. The projectile usually had a silver-colored tip.

Note:

Although the use of the B cartridge as an explosive projectile is mentioned time and again, it was presumably not very common, as the effective range of the projectile ended at around 600 meters.

The Pr cartridge (phosphorus) was used as a further incendiary projectile.

The pointed bullet with a hardened steel core was only produced until 1942 due to the lack of tungsten.

In the case of tracer ammunition, the projectile was combined with a tracer charge. This was ignited by burning nitro powder. The burning time reached up to 900 meters. A so-called glow mark was visible.

Telescopic sight (ZF)

Various models were issued as riflescopes, which differed in mounting, magnification or light intensity. Depending on availability, the riflescopes (e.g. ZF 39, ZF 41, ZF 4) were selected by the shooters according to their needs and preferences.

Loot weapon

The sniper version of the Russian Mosin Nagant, a robust and reliable 5-shot repeating carbine, was a popular weapon for German snipers on the Eastern Front.

Contrary to the German snipers, their Russian counterparts did use explosive bullets. These were used by the German snipers with the prey rifles (if the corresponding ammunition was found) in individual cases as required.

Sniper badge:

The sniper badge, donated by Adolf Hitler on August 8, 1944, was awarded in three stages.

- Level 1 (3rd class) = 20 kills
- Level 2 (2nd class) = 40 kills
- Level 3 (1st class) = 60 kills

It was forbidden to include shots fired in close combat. The enemy was also not allowed to show any intention of defecting or being captured.

All kills had to be confirmed. Snipers sometimes kept a notebook in which they recorded their successes. The following had to be noted: Shot number, place and time, a brief statement of the facts and a witness.

The badge is made of greenish-grey fabric, embroidered several times and oval. It shows a black eagle's head turned to the right with white plumage, an ochre eye and a closed beak. The body is covered by an oak leaf fragment consisting of three leaves and an acorn arranged on the left. The edges of the badge are stitched. The individual levels can be distinguished by the cord sewn around them, in silver for level 2 or gold for level 3.

Snipers were hated and feared by the enemy. On all fronts, snipers who were captured were mistreated or even tortured to death. For this reason, precision marksmen generally refrained from wearing the sniper badge. Notebooks and equipment that could be used to identify a sniper were disposed of when capture was imminent.

Successful sniper of the Waffen-SS and holder of the 3rd level of the sniper badge (1st class):

- *SS-Untersturmführer Otto Willscher*, SS Parachute Infantry Battalion 600
- *SS-Rottenführer Elmo Scheffel*, SS-Fallschirm-Jäger-Bataillon 600

Successful sniper of the Wehrmacht and holder of the 3rd level of the sniper badge (1st class):

- *Private Matthäus Hetzenauer*, 7th Company, Mountain Infantry Regiment 144, 3rd Mountain Division
- *Corporal Josef Allerberger*, 8th Company, Mountain Infantry Regiment 144, 3rd Mountain Division
- *Corporal Josef Roth*, 8th Company, Mountain Infantry Regiment 144, 3rd Mountain Division
- *Private Bruno Sutkus*, Staff II. Battalion, Grenadier Regiment 196, 68th Infantry Division
- *Private Hans Gruber*, 5th Company, Mohr Regiment

Stalingrad 1 – from Sophia Wallenda

List of sources and references

All books in the bibliography are in German.

War Diary of the High Command of the Wehrmacht (Wehrmachtsführungs-stab) 1940-1945 (1961 - 1965) Special Edition, Berdard & Graefe Verlag, Bonn, ed. Prof. Dr. Percy Ernst Schramm, explained by Prof. Dr. Andreas Hillgruber, Prof. Dr. Walther Hubatsch, Prof. Dr. Hans-Adolf Jacobsen and Prof. Dr. Percy Ernst Schramm, ISBN 3-7637-5933-6

Wikipedia according to the inserted links.
The license conditions can be viewed under the following link:
http://creativecommons.org/licenses/by-sa/3.0/deed.de

Infantry Weapons Yesterday (1918-1945) Volume 1
Reiner Lidschun, Günter Wollert, Brandenburgisches Verlagshaus, 3rd edition 1998, ISBN 3-89488-036-8

Infantry Weapons Yesterday (1918-1945) Volume 2
Reiner Lidschun, Günter Wollert, Brandenburgisches Verlagshaus, 3rd edition, 1998, ISBN 3-89488-036-8

Stalingrad, Antony Beevor, Pantheon Verlag, 2nd edition 2010, ISBN 978-3-570-55134-9

Waffen SS snipers on the Eastern Front - Im Fadenkreuz der Jäger, information, original photos and a gripping novel, Books on Demand, ISBN: 978-3-7347-3984-2, January 2015, 132 p., € 8.90, Wolfgang Wallenda

Sniper mission in Voronezh - information, original photos and a gripping novel, Books on Demand, ISBN: 978-3-7357-5629-9, July 2014, 120 p., € 8.90, Wolfgang Wallenda

www.ingramcontent.com/pod-product-compliance
Ingram Content Group UK Ltd.
Pitfield, Milton Keynes, MK11 3LW, UK
UKHW040804210125
453966UK00001B/42